Dr. Nightingale Traps the Missing Lynx

A DEIRDRE QUINN NIGHTINGALE MYSTERY

Lydia Adamson

D0186957

A SIGNET BOOK

SIGNET
Published by the Penguin Group
Penguin Putnam Inc., 375 Hudson Street,
New York, New York 10014, U.S.A.
Penguin Books Ltd, 27 Wrights Lane,
London W8 5TZ, England
Penguin Books Australia Ltd,
Ringwood, Victoria, Australia
Penguin Books Canada Ltd, 10 Alcorn Avenue,
Toronto, Ontario, Canada M4V 3B2
Penguin Books (N.Z.) Ltd, 182–190 Wairau Road,
Auckland 10, New Zealand

Penguin Books Ltd, Registered Offices:
Harmondsworth, Middlesex, England

First published by Signet, an imprint of Dutton NAL, a member of
Penguin Putnam Inc.

First Printing, July 1999
10 9 8 7 6 5 4 3 2

Copyright © Lydia Adamson, 1999
All rights reserved

Ⓟ REGISTERED TRADEMARK—MARCA REGISTRADA

Printed in the United States of America

PUBLISHER'S NOTE
This is a work of fiction. Names, characters, places, and incidents either
are the product of the author's imagination or are used fictitiously, and
any resemblance to actual persons, living or dead, events, or locales is
entirely coincidental.

BOOKS ARE AVAILABLE AT QUANTITY DISCOUNTS WHEN USED TO PROMOTE
PRODUCTS OR SERVICES. FOR INFORMATION PLEASE WRITE TO PREMIUM
MARKETING DIVISION, PENGUIN PUTNAM INC., 375 HUDSON STREET, NEW YORK,
NEW YORK 10014.

Chapter 1

It was a freezing January morning, but even so, at 6 A.M. Dr. Deirdre Quinn Nightingale, DVM, assumed the lotus position on the cold ground. She was performing her yogic breathing exercises, watched as always at a respectful distance by the motley collection of yard dogs.

When she finished she walked into the kitchen and joined another motley crew: the group of household retainers she had long referred to as her elves, who were just sitting down to breakfast. This appearance by the doctor at the breakfast table was most unusual. For Dr. Nightingale, Didi to her friends, never ate breakfast with the elves.

Mrs. Tunney, housekeeper and chief elf, was so surprised that she fumbled the oatmeal spoon. But old Charlie Gravis, the doctor's veterinary assistant, barely looked up, and then went back to staring gloomily into his coffee. Young Trent Tucker, general handyman and chauffeur extraordinaire, found it funny, and broke into an impish grin. And the strangely beautiful golden-haired Abigail, overseer and protector of all the on-premises animals—the yard dogs, the doctor's thoroughbred horse, and Charlie Gravis's pigs—just sat there looking as beatifically vague as ever.

Didi stirred a little brown sugar into her oatmeal. She didn't know quite how to proceed. She wanted to talk to the group about economizing, but she didn't want to alarm them. She knew that her elves did not really trust her as they had trusted her late mother; that they were afraid she would abrogate the unwritten contract that her mother had formed with them—room and board in perpetuity in exchange for basic chores dealing with house and land.

She added a little cream to her bowl and then a little more brown sugar. No one else had touched his oatmeal yet. They were all waiting for her. She had to let them know that it was crunch time. There was a cash flow problem. January and February were always the worst months in a large animal vet's practice. But this year it seemed everything had dried up. And she had not been able to break into that closed circle of the large breeding stables. She knew she had to expand her small animal practice, but was reluctant to open the clinic more than twice a week. Meanwhile, the monthly bills mounted higher and higher. There was the medical insurance for the five of them, and the remaining payments on her Jeep, and monthly payments for the addition to the house which constituted her small animal clinic, and the taxes and the fuel bills and the loan she had taken out to pay for the last two years of vet school. And since she paid the elves no salary whatsoever, she had to purchase winter coats for them as well as clothes for herself. Then there were the skyrocketing feed bills for those pigs and for her horse Promise Me. The weight of it all was beginning to crush her.

Didi ate, at last, a spoonful of oatmeal. Her elves followed suit.

"You want some butter for that?" Charlie asked. As he proffered the plate, the butter knife fell off with a clatter.

"Watch out for that!" Mrs. Tunney barked at him, disapproval tightening her jaw. She replaced the knife primly.

"No, thank you," Didi said.

"The toast is ready," Mrs. Tunney chirped in Didi's direction. "Rye toast this morning."

Again, "No, thank you" from Didi. She ate another spoonful of oatmeal. The tension was becoming unbearable. I am ruining their breakfast, she thought.

She pushed the bowl away, stood, and announced boldly: "I just wanted to tell all of you that I'm going to the hardware store in town this morning."

The elves stared at one another, not knowing what to make of the pronouncement.

"Whatever you need," Didi quickly added, "make a list for me." And with that she hurried out of the kitchen, still carrying her coffee cup. *Tomorrow*, she thought, as she hurried back to her room to shower and dress. I'll discuss it with them tomorrow.

Back in the kitchen, the elves resumed their breakfast.

"What do you make of it?" Mrs. Tunney asked. "Her coming in here like that."

No one replied.

"I asked a question!" Mrs. Tunney announced. "You know Miss Quinn never sits down with us at breakfast."

Charlie finally spoke up. "Guess she was hungry."

Mrs. Tunney made a face. It was obvious she considered that explanation stupid, at best. "I see dark clouds coming," she intoned.

The others continued to eat. Old lady Tunney was always seeing dark clouds coming.

"It's snowing," Charlie Gravis announced as they exited the hardware store with their bundles. It was 11 A.M.

"I am aware of the existing weather conditions," Didi said testily.

Charlie didn't speak again, but he was thinking, You should have ate your oatmeal this morning, young miss. Maybe it would've improved your mood.

"We're going to go to the diner, get some coffee, and call into the machine to see if there's any work," Didi told him.

"Sounds good," he quickly agreed. He always liked the way she spoke about veterinary work. She called it "work." Nothing fancy. Yes, he liked that about the boss.

5

Once at the diner they slid into a choice booth near the window. The place was half-empty—between breakfast and lunch crowds.

Myra, the on-again, off-again waitress, threw the menus down without a word. Her bad manners were legendary but no one seemed to pay her much mind. Didi went and made the call. She was back in less than a minute. "Nothing," she said simply. She and Charlie studied the menu for no reason at all, and then both ordered coffee. Charlie, on second thought, called for a toasted corn muffin, buttered, with marmalade on the side.

After Myra left to deliver the order to the kitchen, Charlie leaned over and whispered: "I hear that she has two husbands."

"Who?"

"Myra. The waitress. One in New Jersey and one in Glen Falls."

"I find that hard to believe, Charlie."

"Well, where do you think she goes when she disappears from here all the time?"

"I have no idea. But she doesn't look to me like the kind of woman who would have two husbands."

Charlie shrugged. "Anyway, if I was the

owner of this diner, I'd have fired her a long time ago."

Myra brought the coffee. Two minutes later she brought the muffin. It was underdone, not nearly crisp enough, but Charlie didn't send it back.

He and Didi watched the snow as it fell. As she sat observing Charlie spread marmalade on the second half of the muffin, Didi heard: "How nice it is to finally meet you!"

She turned toward the booming male voice. Standing next to the booth was a huge fat man wearing a full-length electric-blue down coat and a rather ridiculous Australian bush hat.

"I have heard of your skill as well as your beauty," the big man said. It was only at that moment that she realized he was addressing her. Charlie put the remainder of his muffin back on the plate.

"Allow me to introduce myself," the stranger continued.

Didi knew exactly who the man was; she had seen many photos of him in the local newspapers. He was Hillsbrook's latest celebrity, Buster Purchase. He had become famous as a wacky weatherman at a Los Angles television station and then made a fortune selling roomy American cars in TV ads. He had decided to retire to Hillsbrook, he told the papers, because James Cagney had retired and died in this area and what was good enough for America's greatest tough-guy actor was good enough for him.

Since moving to Hillsbrook he had become a whirlwind. The papers said he had single-handedly resurrected Hillsbrook social life. He gave parties. He raised money for charity. He started all kinds of clubs around his many hobbies, which included American Indian archaeology, the Civil War, cats, and God knew what else. Yes, Didi knew exactly who he was.

After the formal introduction the huge celebrity said, "I was wondering, Dr. Nightingale, whether you would help me with a rather serious problem."

"What problem is that, Mr. Purchase?"

"I just received word that Dr. Corcoran is snowed in at O'Hare Airport in Chicago and won't be able to get back here today. You know Dr. Corcoran?"

"I've heard of him, yes. A fine vet."

"Yes, he is. And he was supposed to be at my fund-raiser today in a professional capacity. We are auctioning off some kittens at my house today. There will be excellent edibles, excellent drink, and the auction is for a very worthy cause."

"Why do you need a vet at a fund-raiser?"

"Well, these are not your ordinary kittens. And I thought it would give the fund-raiser a certain pizazz if a fine vet issued a certificate of health as each kitten is adopted after a healthy donation. You see, as I said, these are not your everyday kittens."

"What type of kittens are they?" Didi asked, now both perplexed and intrigued.

He puffed himself up and said in a rather conspiratorial voice: "*Lynx rufus rufus* Buster."

The young vet burst into laughter. Charlie transferred his look of confusion from Purchase to his boss. Didi said to her assistant when she could control her mirth: "That is the eastern bobcat's scientific name, Charlie." Then she asked Buster Purchase: "Have you bred a new species of bobcat?"

"Not exactly, Dr. Nightingale. The daddy is a wild Michigan bobcat and the mother is a charming Hillsbrook barn cat. The kittens, I might add, are glorious."

"Mr. Purchase, I'm sure the kittens are glorious," Didi replied, "but I don't think you can add your name to *Lynx rufus rufus*. There are many instances of these kinds of hybrids."

With a twinkle in his eye the fat man answered, "Ah, the search for immortality is a difficult one. But will you take Dr. Corcoran's place?"

"It's very short notice," Didi said, "and I think I have an appointment this evening."

"Oh, it's not this evening. It's this afternoon. At four. And it'll all be over by six. I know the fee isn't that much for a vet of your caliber— only five hundred dollars—but you would be helping a very worthy cause."

Didi tensed. Five hundred dollars. She didn't want to do it. But that was a princely sum for next to no work at all. She was, as her mother used to say, between the devil and the deep blue sea.

"Where is your home?" she asked.

Buster Purchase beamed. He gave her precise directions, shook hands with her and with Charlie, expressed his wish that Charlie accompany her this afternoon, and rolled out of the diner.

After Purchase was gone Charlie went back to his muffin. Didi fiddled with her coffee morosely.

"You know, boss," Charlie said after a time, "I would've laid a hundred to one odds that you never would have agreed to do this . . . if I was a betting man, I mean."

Didi stared hard at him. She couldn't be angry with him, she realized. She hadn't told him what she was supposed to have told him and the others at breakfast.

So she smiled and said, "That's why you should never gamble, Charlie." Then she remembered that she had not asked just what Buster Purchase's worthy cause was.

Didi and her assistant arrived at the Purchase home a tad before four. She was astonished at the size of the crowd and the cross section of Hillsbrook it represented.

There were the Napiers and the Cooks—old Hillsbrook hunt people who probably hadn't been to a social event since the hounds and horses abandoned Hillsbrook.

The Mintons were there: he, a banker, she, a physician. And the Woolfs—husband and wife owners of the largest and most profitable dairy operation in the area. There was Jeremy Lukens, who owned the only men's clothing store in town and fancied himself a kind of local cultural czar. And there were a lot of people Didi knew by sight but not by name.

It was most definitely a crowd with money, but Buster Purchase had also invited the derelict poet Burt Conyers and he was there in full regalia including sheepskin vest and staff. Harland Frick was also in attendance. He owned the health food store in town and was Hillsbrook's oral historian.

Didi didn't see her friend Rose Vigdor. She should have just brought her along, she realized, but it was too late now.

A lovely young woman loomed up in front of them. She looked like a fashion model—willowy, pale, with chiseled features and an enormous mane of black hair.

"I'm Sissy Purchase," she announced. "You must be the fabulous Dr. Nightingale."

It has to be his wife, Didi thought, although she's young enough to be his daughter.

Sissy Purchase pulled the vet and her associate to the buffet table and left them there. It was a truly opulent spread that Didi and Charlie looked upon. Gravis dug right in. Didi, deciding to wait a few minutes before eating, walked over to Harland Frick.

"What is this party for, Harland?" she asked directly.

He polished off a stuffed cabbage before answering: "The Magruder barn."

That made sense. Didi nodded approvingly. The Magruder barn was the oldest standing one in Hillsbrook, built about 1740. And it was barely standing. The man who owned the land had died. His estate was in litigation, the barn was crumbling, and something had to be done.

"They're trying to set up a kind of watchdog committee who'll repair it, watch over it, and lobby for it until the state gives it landmark preservation status," Harland explained between bites of onion tart.

"A 'worthy cause' indeed," Didi said, feeling a little better about the whole project.

Buster Purchase then called the assembled to order.

"Children!" he bellowed. "We must proceed. The food, drink, and other frivolities will wait. This fund-raiser has commenced. The auction is afoot. All of you now please repair to the master bedroom."

"Is he joking?" Didi whispered to Harland. "How is this crowd going to fit into their bedroom?"

Frick laughed. "You haven't seen the bedroom."

They all followed instructions, moving in a wave toward the bedroom. It was indeed the largest one Didi had ever seen. Obviously when the Purchases remodeled this old farmhouse, they had broken through walls to make a bedroom that could hold a herd of dairy cows. It was furnished aggressively with chairs and rugs and divans and bookshelves and, in front of the gigantic four-poster, there was a sunken area that functioned as a kind of sitting room.

A glass door on the windowless side of the room revealed that the Purchases had installed a small greenhouse that one could enter from the bedroom or from without.

"Dr. Nightingale!" Buster Purchase called out. "Please take the seat of honor!" He was pointing to the bed, on which was a stack of ornate, specially printed certificates that read:

Certificate of Health
Lynx rufus rufus Buster

Two pens lay on the bed next to the certificates.

"Kinda like signing a peace treaty," Charlie noted under his breath.

Didi reluctantly sat down. She now realized she didn't like this kind of thing at all. It was nonsense. How could she give those kittens a thorough examination so quickly? It couldn't be done. It was a fake . . . showbiz stuff. Silently, she cursed her need for money. But it was too late to back out. She would give Purchase what he wanted—a cursory examination of each cat—eyes, ears, nose, throat, coat, conformation, muscular coordination, and other superficialities.

The Fat Man was in his glory. "I shall now enter the bobcat's lair," he announced gleefully, "which usually functions as our greenhouse. I'll say hello to mamma cat, bring out the babies, and deliver them to good Dr. Nightingale. Upon completion of the exam, bidding will commence."

The guests applauded. Buster Purchase opened the glass door, walked into the greenhouse, and brought out six kittens, three at a time.

He placed them on the bed next to Didi, accompanied by the oohs and aahs of the crowd.

Six sets of kitten eyes looked up at her. They were truly adorable, somewhere between eight and twelve weeks old.

Four of the cats were coal black, resembling domestic kittens except that they had larger feet. The other two had bobtails, tufted ears, big feet, and black dots on charcoal-gray coats.

Didi forgot her distaste for the project. She was charmed out of her boots.

But then all hell broke loose. One kitten jumped onto her shoulder. Two began chasing each other over the pillows. One headed up a post. And the remaining two started ripping up the certificates.

"Surround the bed!" Buster shouted.

A phalanx of guests complied, cordoning off possible exit routes for the kittens. A kind of order was restored.

Didi picked up one kitten at a time, examined it quickly, and signed and dated each certificate, referring to the cats as "Buster One," "Buster Two," and so on.

Then the auction commenced with Buster Purchase serving as auctioneer. Of course, it had nothing to do with kittens and everyone knew it. It had to do with donating money to save the Magruder barn.

The two kittens who looked like their bobcat daddy went fast. One to the Napiers for $2,000. One to the Mintons for $1,600.

The rest of the litter, who resembled their barn cat mother, moved more slowly. And in the end only two were taken. One to Jeremy Lukens for $500. One to a woman Didi did not know for $360.

Then Purchase declared the fund-raiser over—it was time to do some serious eating and drinking.

"Doctor," he said, "please distribute the certificates to the lucky parties. I shall return the two remaining kittens to their mother who I assure you thinks they have been slighted."

Appreciative laughter all around.

Didi was astonished. Almost $5,000 raised in five minutes—in a bedroom! She handed a certificate to each of the bidders, not at all sure which cat was Buster One and which was Buster Four.

Well, what did it matter?

Buster Purchase vanished into the greenhouse with the two kittens, leaving the glass door slightly ajar.

Sissy began shepherding the guests back into the living room, including the winners who had their newly acquired bobcat hybrids and certificates in their arms.

"I can use a little help in here, Sissy," they heard Buster call.

"Be there in a second," replied his wife, busy at the moment with the poet, a bit soused, who had caught his sheepskin vest on an expensive floor lamp.

By the time she had disengaged Burt Conyers, it wasn't necessary to go to her husband's assistance. He had walked out of the greenhouse.

Someone screamed.

Buster's face and neck were lined with deep, bloody scratches.

He smiled idiotically. Then he fell forward. He was dead when he hit the ground.

Mrs. Minton rushed to him. Others ran around in a panic, searching for the phone. Sissy Purchase stood where she was, wavering, swaying on her feet as if she were about to topple over. Her hands were all tangled up in her lustrous raven hair.

Didi approached the lifeless body on the floor. Mrs. Minton was dutifully performing CPR—but to no avail.

Up close, Buster's wounds were puffy and discolored.

Didi's eyes went to the half-opened door of

the greenhouse. She walked quickly over to it and shut the door tightly. Then she stationed herself there like an embassy guard and listened to the sounds of a party disintegrating. She felt calm, but it was as though everything was happening in another dimension.

Only three things seemed clear:

Buster Purchase was dead.

It had to have been the mother cat who delivered the ugly scratches to the wacky weatherman's face and neck.

What had entered Buster's wounds—what had killed him—had all the earmarks of rattlesnake venom.

Chapter 2

"What is the matter with you, Rose? You swore to me you were going to get some kind of heating system installed. How can you live like this?"

Didi stamped her feet on the ground and pulled her collar tight. Around her feet ran Huck, Rose Vigdor's little Corgi, and Rose's two German shepherds, Aretha and Bozo. Only five minutes ago she had been unwise enough to give them all dog bones, and now they would not let her rest.

Rose, who was wrapped up in what appeared to be at least twenty mufflers, just grinned. The winter wind whipped through the huge shell of a barn that was Rose's "bucolic" home. She pointed to the small potbellied stove near the sliding doors.

"A mosquito couldn't get warm by that fire," Dr. Nightingale noted.

"Oh, you vets are all the same. Always complaining."

"I'm not complaining, Rose. I'm just pointing out that there're at least two more months of winter left. But I assure you I shall look after your beasts when pneumonia pays you a visit."

One shaft of morning sun was suddenly cutting a wide swath through the barn.

"You see," Rose said gleefully, "it will heat up soon. By noon this place will be warm as toast." She pulled the dogs away from Didi. "You were there yesterday afternoon, weren't you? You saw everything?"

"You mean what happened at the Purchases'?"

"Of course I mean that. What else? The man died right in front of you, didn't he?"

"I suppose you can say he did."

"Well, don't just stand there looking at a sunbeam. Tell me what happened."

Didi moved closer to the potbellied stove. Like always, there was a kettle of water boiling over the grate. In a minute Rose would be able to brew a pot of her infamous herbal tea. Rose lived on tea and assorted chips.

"It was strange and it was sad," Didi said.

"I was at the diner early this morning and people were saying that it was more than just 'strange.'"

"The man died of a heart attack, Rose. Charlotte Minton was right there."

"Is that the woman who used to be a GP?"

"Right. Now she just does some consulting in pediatrics. She tried to revive him. No use. The man was dead when he hit the ground."

"So why is the buzz going around?"

"Well, it turned out there were scratch marks on his face. He had brought the two kittens he couldn't sell back to mamma cat. She must have scratched him. I don't know why. He came back outside and fell down dead. And that was that. What was strange were the scratch marks."

"Common enough."

"Yes. But the wounds were puffy and discolored. As if he'd been bitten by a rattler."

"Even I know rattlesnake bites don't look like cat scratches."

"You're right. And that's the problem. A cat scratch acting like a rattler bite."

"There aren't any rattlesnakes around here."

"Not anymore. North and west, in the Catskills, you'll find a few timber rattlers. But they're very rare."

"I'm sorry he's dead, but I never liked the man."

"I didn't realize you knew him."

"I didn't, really. But he blew into town like this combination of Jesse James and Donald Trump. Throwing money around. Starting lecture series. Buying up property. Like a fat Walt Disney character."

"That's unkind, Rose."

"Am I wrong? Didn't he sell four kittens for almost five thousand dollars? You were there. You tell me."

"It was for a fund to save the Magruder farmhouse."

"I don't care what it was for. Look, Didi, there were plenty of people in this town who hated him."

"I could use some tea, Rose."

"And what kind of kittens were they? I hear some kind of weird mixed breed. People like the jolly Fat Man always have to tamper with Mother Nature."

Didi didn't reply.

"I guess you want to change the subject," said Rose. She set about making the tea and handed a mug to her friend. "Anyway, I'd be delighted to change the subject. I'd rather talk about another man."

"You mean Allie Voegler."

"Yes. I mean Allie."

Didi warmed her fingers on the sides of the cup and savored the hot tea. She and Allie had been lovers. They had become engaged. There had been one of those terrible fights and the engagement was broken off. Allie had sort of gone around the bend. After all, the breakup had occurred right after the young Hillsbrook cop Wynton Chung had been murdered. Allie had blamed Didi in a way for the tragedy. And himself. The denouement had been ugly. Officer Voegler had assaulted a witness in the state troopers' barracks. He was promptly suspended. Now he lived out of county, in Cooperstown, undergoing department-ordered psychotherapy. Didi called him from time to time and met him once a week, halfway between Cooperstown and Hillsbrook, in a donut shop on Route 28.

"There's nothing to tell," Didi said after a long, deliberate pause. She wasn't lying to

Rose. But even if there had been some new development, and even though the blond nature girl was her best friend in Hillsbrook, she probably would not confide in Rose right now. Rose was just a bit too sophisticated, a bit too experienced with men, a bit too cynical.

"Do you still love the idiot?"

"Don't call him that, Rose."

"Okay. Do you still love Detective Albert Voegler, late of the Hillsbrook Police Department—tall—handsome—so macho he shaves in cold water, when he does shave—so kindly that when he hunts deer he never puts a bullet into the creature unless he's less than a hundred yards away—so mentally balanced that he gets roaring drunk on two bottles of ale."

Didi waited a long time before answering. Then she said quietly, "Do you know where I was this morning? Before I came here?"

"No."

"At Prathers."

"Who is Prathers?"

"It's a big dairy operation about thirty miles out of town. Their milk goes to the yogurt factory in Binghampton. And they only call me if their regular vet is out of town or busy and it's an emergency."

"Okay. So what does that have to do with Allie?"

"Two of the cows were sick. Anorectic, depressed, coughing, ugly nasal discharge. The foreman tells me it's pneumonia. I tell him it's not really—it's bronchial pneumonia *secondary* to BRSV. He doesn't know what BRSV is. Thinks it's all mumbo jumbo. I tell him it's a virus spread by aerosol droplets. He says, 'Show me.' I say I really can't show him, because the virus is tricky. Attempts to isolate it from nasal swabs are futile. He is very skeptical. I ignore him. I tell him what has to be done. He says, 'Let me clear it with the boss.' He makes a few calls. I wait there staring at the sick cows. He comes back and agrees to follow my instructions."

"I still don't understand what this has to do with anything."

"I'm just trying to make a simple point, Rose."

"Which is?"

"Which is that, just like there are some viruses you can't isolate on a nasal swab, there are some men you can't identify by the way they shave."

Rose burst into laughter. She picked up Huck in her arms and whirled around with him. "Did you hear that, doggie? Now, I ask you, isn't Nightgown the hippest country girl you ever met?"

The two old men sat uncomfortably in a booth in the new Hillsbrook Pub, right on Main Street. It was the first bar to open in Hillsbrook proper in a long time. Oh, there were plenty of other taverns in the area, but they were on the roads leading in and out of town. They served the farmers and the tradesmen and the telephone men and the highway crews.

This new pub obviously was aimed at a different crowd. It looked and felt and smelled like a hotel bar—plenty of leather seats and booths. Obviously this new place was not intended to attract dairy farmers; there weren't many of those left in the Hillsbrook area, anyway. But the elderly man seated across from Charlie Gravis was one of them. His name was Ike Badian and he still had a working dairy operation—small, and steadily shrinking, but still viable.

Charlie began to muse on the possible clientele. "I believe they're going to get the skiers in here."

"No real skiing around here," Ike noted, pulling on a blunt, ugly little cigar, biting off an end, spitting it out, then sucking deeply and sending billows of smoke upward.

"I mean," Charlie said sharply, "skiers on their way to the Catskills or the Berkshires."

"That makes sense. But who's gonna come here in the summer?"

"Tourists," said Charlie.

"I was in town a few times last summer. Didn't see many of them."

"Oh, they're here. You just got to keep your eyes open to spot them."

A young man delivered two steins of ale with a beautiful cap of foam on each. Ike Badian spun his glass around in appreciation. Then he said to his friend: "How come you're not working? Where's your boss?"

"She dropped me in town, then went out to see that friend of hers, the Vigdor girl."

"What about her rounds? This time of day . . . hell, Charlie, it's only a little past twelve noon. You people are supposed to be out on the road sticking needles in poor cows and then leaving some crazy bill for the farmer, who might not have been as poor as the damn cow before you and that Nightingale showed up, but he'll be a poor fool if he pays the damn bill."

"You don't know what you're talking about. The young lady is fair . . . damn fair."

"If you say so, Charlie. But the way I see Dutchess County now is, too many vets and not enough cows."

Charlie leaned over and whispered conspiratorially to his friend: "She's hurting, Ike."

"I figured she was. I figured that was the only reason in hell she's dragging you along to the Fat Man's party." Ike drank some ale, wiped his lips, stuck his cigar back into his mouth. "That party killed him. It must have been wild, eh, Charlie?"

"The best food I ate in a long time."

They sat in silence for a while. Then Ike asked, "That slick red Jeep of hers paid for?"

"Don't think so. Don't think anything's paid for."

"She's feeding a whole lot of mouths."

"And I'm one of them."

"Yeah, you are."

"I've been thinking that I gotta do something, Ike."

"Look, Charlie, you're my friend. And you were a helluva cowman. But that's all over. And let's face it—your moneymaking schemes don't make money. They make trouble. Your doc has enough trouble."

Gravis made no reply to Ike's remark, which was an insult—a playful one from a well-meaning friend, perhaps, but an insult nonetheless.

Didi was leafing through a travel magazine in the village stationery store when she noticed the two men staring at her from outside. She knew one of them. He was Thomas Brasco, the Hillsbrook cop who was temporarily filling in for Allie Voegler as the only plainclothes detective on the eight-man Hillsbrook police force. The other man she did not recognize. He was in suit and tie with a muffler. Brasco motioned through the glass that she should wait there.

The two men entered the store and approached her. Brasco introduced her to his companion as Dr. Nightingale, and then added that she was a "good friend" of Allie's. She didn't particularly like the way he used the term. The companion was introduced to her as Denham Taylor, a state trooper homicide detective.

Brasco did all the talking.

"Allie told me you have a peculiar kind of gift, Doctor. I mean, when it comes to homicide."

"What do you mean?" Didi asked. "Has someone been murdered?"

"Buster Purchase. Maybe."

"Maybe?"

"We think we know what happened yesterday afternoon."

"Good. I was there and I haven't the foggiest idea what happened. Tell me."

"The man had a massive coronary."

"That's how it looked to me," she affirmed.

"In fact, he had a heart condition for many years. A severe one, apparently. But he had refused surgery and was being treated—ostensibly—with diet and drugs."

"So?"

Brasco didn't answer.

"You mean the scratch wounds?" she pressed him.

"We do."

"And the venom?"

"How did you know that?"

"I know what snake bite looks like, Brasco. But Purchase wasn't bitten. He was scratched."

"Yes, and there was venom in the wounds. Charlotte Minton took some scrapings. It was confirmed. Rattlesnake venom."

Didi nodded. "It had to be something like that. The discoloration and swelling are distinctive."

Denham Taylor spoke for the first time: "There is a possibility that someone coated the cat's claws with the venom. Purchase walked back into the greenhouse, was scratched, and the poison worked fast on an already weak heart."

Brasco jumped in then. "Does that make sense to you, Didi?"

"Sense and nonsense."

Brasco did not appear to like that response. He raised his voice and spoke sternly. "No. Not nonsense. Plausible. The man had a very bad heart. He gets scratched by venomous claws. The poison induced a fatal heart attack. What's so unbelievable about that?"

"Look," she said with some exasperation, "if the man had a really severe heart condition, anything could have triggered an attack. Why don't you autopsy him? That might get you something definite."

"Sissy Purchase had the body picked up late last night from the hospital," Brasco said. "The body's on its way back to California. Since the man had a bad heart, and since he died of a coronary, no one ever thought of homicide, scratches aside. We were too late."

"Okay. Look, I'm not an expert on snake bite. But I do know that a healthy man would definitely not die that quicky from a rattler bite. A *healthy* man, I said. I don't think there're a whole lot of studies done on the relation between snake venom and heart disease. Sure, it's possible the venom induced the fatal coronary. Rattlers are pit vipers, and their venom is hemotoxic, necrotizing, anticoagulant, and often neurotoxic."

"So," Taylor noted, "it could have been homicide."

She placed the travel magazine back on the rack. "If it was homicide, then you are dealing with an unbalanced, vengeful individual. There are so many ways to kill someone. Particularly someone with a bad heart. To plan a murder like this—especially during a huge party—seems incredibly bizarre. It would mean that the murderer, for his own reasons and for his own satisfaction, had to kill Buster Purchase in that particular way. A cruel, sick, and very complicated way."

Brasco snorted. "So what else is new?"

"Above all," Didi continued, "it would be an extremely chancy way to kill someone. The whole thing depended on a cat scratching a man at a particular time. But Buster had taken the whole litter away from the mamma cat in the greenhouse and brought each one to me. Was he scratched at that time? No. But when he makes a second trip and gives the mother cat back two of her kittens who weren't sold— then she attacks. Who could arrange things so perfectly? How could the murderer know the cat would scratch at the right time? It just doesn't make any sense."

The state trooper with the muffler gave Dr. Nightingale a long hard look, almost a glare. She returned it.

"I hear a lot of people hated that fat man," Brasco said. "And I hear a lot of people loved him. But no one told me why, either way."

"I can't help you there," Didi replied. "I didn't know him at all."

The two men walked out together without saying a word in parting.

Didi felt suddenly very weary. She plucked another magazine from the rack. This one was a fashion magazine and it featured the coming spring line from France. She leafed through the pages, looking but not seeing. Then she carefully replaced the magazine on the rack, put her hood up, and went to collect Charlie Gravis from the pub.

Albert Voegler sat unhappily in the waiting room of the psychiatric wing of Bassett Hospital outside Cooperstown, New York.

He didn't like the idea that his psychiatric appointment, his therapy, took place inside the walls of a hospital. He didn't like the fact that he was about to meet yet another new shrink—his third. Oh yes, he understood the reason for the venue and the changes. This program to help "disturbed" police officers was a state-funded one, administered jointly by the medical profession and the police union. He understood, but he still didn't like it. Nor in fact would he ever think of himself as a "disturbed" policeman.

Allie rolled and unrolled the magazine in

his hands. It was the most recent issue of *Sports Afield*, the subscription having been a Christmas present from Dr. Nightingale. Who emphatically did not like hunting, but, unlike her friend Rose, did not hate hunters. After all, the deer population was exploding. If they were not culled by the gun, they'd be culled by the automobile—run over on all the highways and byways of Hillsbrook. Maybe even by bicycles. He leaned back in his chair. Yes, Didi had told him: "If I were a deer, I'd rather be killed quickly, by a round in the head, than lay broken and bleeding in the road."

He nodded vigorously as he remembered the conversation. She was smart, all right, Dr. Nightingale. She was humane. She was practical. And God, he missed her so much. They'd have had their regular meeting in that stupid donut shop on Route 28—one of their strained weekly get-togethers—if it weren't for all the commotion in Hillsbrook right now.

Allie shifted his weight in the chair, removed his wallet, and slipped out the dog-eared photograph he had of Didi.

She didn't know he had it. She did not like people taking and keeping photos of her.

He studied the snapshot: the good Dr. Nightingale in a pasture, surrounded by a herd of goats.

He never remembered the breed name of those goats; just that they were exotic. Deirdre was just standing there. It was springtime. She was wearing her beat-up rounds jeans and a sweatshirt. Short dark hair. Wiry. Very pretty face, but with an oddly clenched jaw, as if she were about to interrogate the goats. She carried a small shovel in one hand and a coil of rope around one shoulder. The shovel was to inspect goat droppings. The rope was to hold and secure whatever goat she wanted to examine.

Where was the goat herder? And where was Charlie Gravis? Allie couldn't remember why he hadn't included them in the picture. He couldn't even remember where and why he had snapped it.

He slid the photograph back into the wallet and pocketed it.

Allie was watching the door. The shrink, he knew, would pop his head—or would it be a woman?—out of that door soon and summon him inside. Of course the summons would only bring him into another waiting room. So it went in psychiatric hospitals, whether one was an outpatient or an inpatient.

He unrolled the magazine and studied a few shotgun ads, then rolled it up again and began to slap it against his knee to some interior rhythm.

He realized he felt better physically than he had in a long time. No booze. Not even a lite beer. No tobacco. Not even a puff on a cigar. And he had even started to run a little in the mornings, and do a few sit-ups.

When he had heard the news of the Fat Man's death on the radio that morning, he had hoped he would get a call from Chief Gough . . . telling him to come home . . . saying all was forgiven . . . saying that Allie Voegler's help was needed.

But no call had come in.

Now he knew it never would.

It didn't matter that this was the biggest event to hit Hillsbrook in a long time, the mysterious death of a famous TV weatherman.

It didn't matter that the national media would descend on Hillsbrook.

It didn't matter that Allie was really the only experienced homicide detective Hillsbrook ever had.

No, none of that mattered. He would stay in Cooperstown for the time being . . . and get shrunk.

He stopped drumming the mag against his leg. He, for one, would miss that Fat Man. Buster Purchase, to Allie's mind, had been a huge burst of fresh lunatic air. Why anyone would hate Buster for his antics, much less want to kill him, was inconceivable. Allie grinned as he remembered seeing Purchase during the last hunting season. The Fat Man was at a stand, surrounded by guides, carrying a magnificent imported rifle and dressed like a nineteenth-century French aristocrat hunting elk in Wyoming. It was an outlandish outfit. So what?

Allie grinned even more broadly when he suddenly recalled what the principal of Hillsbrook High had told him a long time ago. Allie, on a bet, had driven his motorcycle up the steps of the school and into the hall. "Son," the principal had said, "only the rich can be eccentric. The poor are crazy." Then he had suspended Allie for the remainder of the term.

The doorknob was turning now. Allie forgot about the Fat Man, Deirdre Quinn Nightingale, and just about everybody else. He rose

quickly, trying to give the impression of therapeutic eagerness.

Charlie Gravis lay fully clothed on his bed.
It was 10:30 P.M. He never fell asleep until
around midnight, and in winter he never took
his clothes off until he was almost under.

His was a tiny bedroom without windows.
The light in the room came from a floor lamp
shaped like a candelabra and activated by a
tasseled string. The lamp, older than the
house, was constantly shorting out.

Charlie was reading a library book with the
aid of his magnifying glasses. He tended to
read only on winter nights, and his current
taste was for biographies of sea captains, pi-
rates, and explorers. The public library had
plenty of such books, and the librarian accom-
modated him eagerly because she found it fas-
cinating that an old dairy farmer would be so
taken with stories about the sea. She often
speculated as to whether sailors were, in turn,
interested in stories about farm life.

Sometimes she teased old Charlie about
that, asking him if he knew any sea chanties
and would he favor her with a few selections.
Charlie always played along, saying he knew

a great many, but the lyrics were much too ribald for the ears of so fine a lady.

The book he was currently reading was a biography of Captain Cook. It was slow going; he had been at it for two weeks now. But he slogged on, anticipating the end, which promised to make very exciting, if grisly reading, as it concerned the murder of Cook by South Sea Islanders.

"Charlie!"

He looked up, startled, and saw Mrs. Tunney in the doorway. He had not even heard the door open. Charlie placed the book down on his chest and cast a hurt expression at the old lady, signaling that she should really have knocked first.

Mrs. Tunney ignored the silent critique of her manners.

"You're going to have to pick the boy up," she pronounced.

He did not have to ask who she meant. "If he fell down, let him pick himself up," Charlie replied, frankly tired of Trent Tucker's shenanigans.

"Not funny. He's out at a place on Route Twenty-six and the pickup's broken down."

"What you really mean is, the kid had three beers and can't see straight."

"I mean exactly what I say, Gravis."

"What's he doing out on Twenty-six? Why ain't he at his usual dive?"

"Now, how should I know that? But Miss Quinn says you can take her Jeep."

"What's the name of the place?"

"Three Stooges . . . if you can imagine that. Miss Quinn says she's heard of it. She says it's a comedy club."

"Or a stripper joint," Charlie muttered.

"What!"

"I'm going, I'm going."

Mrs. Tunney went away. Charlie threw on his big parka with the fur-trimmed hood, changed into boots, and headed out.

Twenty minutes later he pulled into the parking lot of the Three Stooges, which was housed in an ugly one-story cinder-block structure.

The words THREE STOOGES were spelled out in neon letters with a neon mallet in the background. Charlie was astonished at the number of vehicles on the lot so late on a cold night. He spotted Trent Tucker's heap as he walked to the entrance.

The moment he walked inside he ran into difficulty. A young woman at a high desk demanded a five-dollar admission fee. Charlie didn't have five dollars on him.

"Now, listen," he said. "First of all, I'm a senior citizen. Second of all, I'm just here to pick up my grandson."

The latter statement was a bald-faced lie. Trent Tucker was, at best, a very distant cousin.

The young woman said she'd settle for $2.50. Charlie paid and walked on, looking for his "grandson." The bar was throbbing with people. Tucker wasn't among them. Charlie moved into the main area and saw him seated at a small table against the wall, only a few feet from the stage. There were two empty beer bottles in front of him.

Charlie moved heavily into the seat beside the younger man.

"Thanks for coming," said Trent. "The damn thing just conked out on me. I'll get someone to take a look at it tomorrow."

"Let's get out of here."

"In a minute, Charlie. One more."

"One more what?"

"Comic."

Gravis shook his head grimly. What a fool this boy was.

A moment later a woman walked onto the stage wearing a purple jumpsuit. She was thin as a rail. Her reddish-blond hair was frizzled and stuck out on all sides, like a rag doll's.

She began to speak in a deadpan voice about the night she lost her virginity—in the back of a pickup truck in Onandaga County.

Never once did she crack a smile, but the audience was howling and applauding.

Charlie didn't move a muscle. He was in shock. Never in his life had he heard such explicit language about the sexual act. He could not believe what he was hearing. The routine got wilder and wilder. Some customers seemed to be on the verge of rolling on the floor, so great was their mirth.

But Charlie Gravis couldn't share in the laughter. A slow, disabling blush was crawling up his body. He looked over at Trent Tucker. The young man, between guffaws, was banging an empty beer bottle on the table after every punch line. He looked like a wild coyote chasing a rabbit.

Finally the act was over. Tucker leaned back against the wall, grinning. "Well, old man, I ask you . . . is that one funny lady or what?"

Charlie said nothing. He got slowly to his feet and walked toward the door. Trent followed him all the way out to the red Jeep with a kind of skipping gait.

Gloomy, gloomy night, Didi thought as she sat on what had been her mother's rocker in what had been her mother's bedroom, with one of her mother's shawls wrapped around her shoulders.

What a difference a year makes. Twelve months ago she was on top of the world. Her practice was booming, and she and Allie were on cloud nine—so in love.

Now the bottom had dropped out of her life.

She closed her eyes and rocked. On the ancient record player was one of her mother's old favorites: Chopin mazurkas. The music seemed to make Didi colder. She often played her mother's old records, even the ones she did not like. It was her way of communicating with the dead.

Suddenly there was a noise coming from

outside, at the front of the house. She wondered if Charlie had returned with Trent Tucker and was now being lectured by Mrs. Tunney for some indiscretion.

The noise grew louder. Didi walked out of the bedroom and stood at the top of the stairs listening. Yes, that was Mrs. Tunney's voice, and she did indeed seem to be shouting at someone. But it was at too high a decibel for Charlie to be the recipient. There was a fierce anger and real threat in her voice.

Didi rushed downstairs and out of the front door, and was immediately hit by a blast of cold wind. What she saw was so incredible that she had to take a moment to steady herself.

Mrs. Tunney was standing near the road with Charlie's shotgun in her hand. She was screaming at gaunt, bearded Burt Conyers, who stood on the other side of the road, resplendent in his shaggy sheepskin, looking very much like John the Baptist.

Didi ran to the older woman's side. "What is going on here, Mrs. Tunney? Put that gun down!"

"If he throws another rock at this house, Miss Quinn, I'm going to blow his head off," Mrs. Tunney retorted.

Didi stepped directly in front of her, pushing the barrel of the shotgun downward. She called out to Conyers: "Are you throwing rocks?"

He executed a long, low, languorous bow in the Elizabethan fashion, then he fell, recovered, and started to bow again.

Dr. Nightingale was not amused. She knew he was the town's newly discovered hero: a crazy, talented derelict. She knew he had recently achieved a local and even national reputation as a poet, as a kind of noir Robert Frost. She knew that he was starting to be anthologized. And that academics were beginning to write theses on him. She even liked a few of his poems.

But she also knew him as a dangerous, manipulative drunk.

"What do you think you're doing, Burt?" Didi demanded.

"Madame," he shouted back, "I am merely enforcing a mourning period for the virtuous Buster Purchase. I am walking through the village of Hillsbrook and stoning houses with lights burning. To pay proper respect to the departed, I have decreed total darkness."

"Get out of here—now!" she responded.

"He died for you!" Conyers protested, then raised one arm.

Mrs. Tunney tried to lift the shotgun, struggling against Didi's grip on the barrel.

Just then, the red Jeep zoomed out of the darkness and braked. Its headlights illuminated the wild-looking poet. Trent Tucker jumped out from the passenger side. Conyers began to laugh, and then shuffled off into the darkness.

Didi was trembling from the encounter, and from the frigid air. She did not wait around to explain to Trent and Charlie. Mrs. Tunney could do that. She ran back into the house, up the stairs, and into her bedroom, slamming the door behind her.

The Chopin record was still playing. She stopped the disk with such force that she broke the needle housing.

Chapter 3

Six A.M. The breakfast partita in the Nightingale household commenced. Mrs. Tunney, doing a little arthritic dance in front of the stove to get warm, was preparing the oatmeal and coffee. Charlie Gravis and Trent Tucker had not yet arrived. Abigail was there as usual, giving the old woman moral support. She sat on a high kitchen stool, shivering and humming, one hand pulling at her long golden hair

"Set the table, child," Mrs. Tunney ordered.

Abigail slipped off the seat and began to place the saucers, cups, plates, and silverware. She carried out her duties slowly, fastidiously.

Mrs. Tunney walked to the window and peered out into the yard, still gray from the slow-fading night. "Would you believe she's out there in this weather! Sitting right on the ground, doing that Chinese nonsense."

"It's not nonsense," Abigail replied pleasantly. "It's yoga. And it doesn't come from China. It's from India."

"It don't matter a bit where it comes from. It'll give the miss pneumonia or worse," Mrs. Tunney noted, shaking her head sadly and going back to her stove.

Outside, Didi, in the lotus position, began the last phase of her yogic breathing exercise. Her body ached from the cold and her feet were totally numb, but she never for a moment thought of aborting the yoga regimen.

She closed her left nostril and began to inhale slowly through her right, counting silently.

Then she began to exhale to the same beat. Just as she was about to begin inhaling from the left nostril, she saw the shadow.

It had loomed up and frightened her so badly that she fell backward out of the lotus position. Quickly she scrambled to all fours.

The thought came to her that Burt Conyers had returned.

"I'm sorry if I frightened you," Sissy Purchase said.

Didi stood up, confused. The visitor was now bathed in light from the kitchen window. Didi's impression of Purchase's wife at the party had been that the young woman looked like a fashion model. But fashion models were rather vacuous as a rule. No, Sissy Purchase was much more beautiful and not at all vacuous-looking. She was very tall, but not frighteningly thin, with wide shoulders. In fact she was breathtaking; like an elegant, feral, black-maned Amazon.

"Don't you remember me?" she pressed. "Some people call me Sissy. But my name is Samantha. I didn't plan on surprising you like this. I parked up the road. I didn't think anyone would be up . . . but then I saw the light . . . then I saw you."

She handed Didi an envelope. "I was planning to slip it under the door."

"What is this?"

"The five hundred dollars Buster owed you for vetting the kittens. I'm leaving Hillsbrook later in the morning. The moving vans will be at my place in about an hour."

Didi opened the envelope. There were five hundred-dollar bills inside it. "Thank you."

The beautiful woman turned and began to walk away.

"Just a moment," Didi called.

"Yes?"

"I am very sorry about your husband."

Mrs. Purchase nodded. "He should not have died like that," she said.

"Like what?"

Samantha Purchase did not answer. Nor did she move again.

"What was that you were saying, about the moving vans?" asked Didi.

"I am closing down the house *now*. I am getting *out* of Hillsbrook. I'm getting *away*—as far and as fast as I can." She smiled sadly then. "I think you know why, Dr. Nightingale. Because everyone in this town hated us."

"That's ridiculous. That's not true."

"Isn't it? Someone once threw a dead woodchuck through our garage window. And then there was the pig blood poured all over Buster's car upholstery. And what about all those young men who made obscene phone calls to us in the middle of the night?"

"Did you report those incidents to the police?" Didi asked, finding the whole harassment scenario very hard to believe.

"Don't be silly!"

Samantha "Sissy" Purchase turned and started off again.

"Wait!" Didi shouted, but this time her visitor did not turn back.

Dr. Nightingale stood dumbfounded in the yard, holding the envelope. There was one critical question she should have asked and didn't: Do you believe your husband was murdered?

She walked into the house. All her elves were at the table, partaking.

"The coffee's hot," Mrs. Tunney said.

Didi picked a cup from the dish rack and poured some.

"Can you imagine that Burt Conyers!" Mrs. Tunney blurted out. It was obvious that no one inside had been aware of the visitor outside the kitchen window only a few minutes before.

"He was drunk," Trent Tucker offered.

"You should know," Charlie noted wickedly.

"I should have put some buckshot into him," Mrs. Tunney said. "And believe me, the next time—"

Her rundown of the vengeance she would wreak on the poet was interrupted when Abigail, for some reason, began to recite one of Conyers's morbid poems—the one, in fact, that had brought him recognition at this rather late time in his life:

Behold the wildflowers
Those sweet carpets of death.
Suck in their sweet strychnine
pollen!

Further recitation was prevented by a very angry Mrs. Tunney, who raised her voice and spoke sharply to Abigail—something she rarely did. "For God's sake, save me from that crazy man's poems."

"Yeah, specially at breakfast," added Trent.

Didi opened the envelope, extracted one of the hundred-dollar bills, rather crisp it was, and laid it down gently on the middle of the kitchen table. "Get yourselves some warm gloves," she said. "All of you. Winter has a long way to go."

They all stared silently at the gift, not knowing what to say.

Didi walked upstairs to her bedroom and sat down on the rocker, sipping the black coffee. Samantha a.k.a. Sissy Purchase had unnerved the doctor.

First of all, there was her wild beauty, something that had simply been hidden at the party. It was as if she had two selves which could be zippered in along with a clothes change.

But her accusations were even more perplexing. A low-grade terror campaign against the jovial, kindly Fat Man? Why? True, Rose Vigdor disliked him. And probably many others did too. But what really were their reasons other than an aversion to ostentation . . . a dislike of new money coming into town and being spent unwisely? There was no doubt about it. The Fat Man had been wildly ostentatious. He did throw money around. He did found a club that dug for Indian artifacts. He did buy books for the library in honor of his Civil War Reading Society, or whatever it was called. He did give money to the hospital for vending machines that dispensed free hot chocolate in the waiting room. He did breed bobcats and domestic cats and auction the progeny for a committee to save the Magruder farm. He did wear ridiculous clothing. He did sponsor wine tastings. He did give radio interviews outlining elaborate, outlandish, impossible schemes for lowering the very high unemployment rate in Dutchess County.

So?

Maybe Mrs. Purchase was still in shock. Maybe she had simply blown up a few tiny incidents into a campaign of rural terror.

Maybe.

Didi finished her coffee, showered, and dressed for work. The problem was, there was no work that morning. She went into the barn and began to groom her horse Promise Me, a task usually performed by Abigail.

Then the young doctor took a walk around her property, trying to evaluate which parcels of land she could sell if the cash crunch worsened . . . and whether or not she could expect to find a buyer given the depressed real estate market.

Finally, she got into the Jeep and drove off. Five minutes into her spin she realized that she wasn't out on just a random drive. She knew exactly where she was going, and why. She was going to the Purchase house because in her heart she simply could not believe that Sissy was abandoning Hillsbrook so precipitously—lock, stock, and barrel.

The moment she pulled up to the sprawling house she realized that Mrs. Buster Purchase had been telling the truth. Even from the road she could tell that the movers had been there.

The bare windows revealed that the house had indeed been cleared out—not a stick of furniture remained.

She pulled the Jeep into the driveway and circled the house by foot, peering in through the windows. It was a ghostly spectacle. The only objects left inside appeared to be unused packing crates and a few unwanted, rolled-up rugs.

Once at the back of the place, she studied the small greenhouse carefully. It was a beautifully built addition to the bedroom, and like the rest of the house, was now empty.

No plants. No mamma cat and kittens.

She opened the outside greenhouse door and moved it back and forth on its hinge. If indeed someone had coated the cat's claws with venom, it would have been quite easy to do, from the outside as well as the inside. Just open the door, walk in, do it, and walk out. Given the hubbub of the auction in the bedroom, no one would have heard a thing.

But there was a problem with this scenario. Venom loses its potency very quickly in the open air. Therefore, the person in question would have had to know approximately when Buster was going to return to the greenhouse with the two unauctioned kittens. How could anyone know that? Even Buster himself.

She walked back and forth in front of the three-sided glass edifice, sloshing through the mud and snow.

She heard the sound of a car engine. A strange-looking van had pulled onto the Purchase property on the far side of the house—approaching through a field rather than the road. It pulled to within fifty feet of the entrance and then stopped. There were antennae sticking out of the top of the vehicle and three people squeezed into the front seat. Now Didi could see the NBC on the side of the vehicle. My, my, she thought, Hillsbrook is about to get a little dose of fame and notoriety, thanks to the late Fat Man.

She headed back toward her own vehicle. Just as she was turning the corner her eye caught a dull patch at the bottom of the greenhouse glass. She walked back over, kicked the slush away, and squatted down.

She ran her hand over the glass two or three times, then stood up and began to walk fast, very fast, to her car phone.

* * *

Cassius Bottoms was the automotive genius Trent Tucker had selected to deal with his stranded pickup. The ride to the Three Stooges parking lot was giving Charlie Gravis a headache. Bottoms was driving his own pickup, with Trent Tucker beside him and Charlie Gravis wedged in at the window seat. The freckled, red-haired friend of Trent's played horrendous music all during the drive; it sounded like dogs with cymbals chasing cows with snare drums.

But once they reached the lot, Cassius fairly leaped into the fray . . . half-vanishing into the maw of Trent's wounded truck.

Charlie and Trent stood a few feet away, watching and stamping their feet to keep warm.

"I hope he knows what the hell he's doing," Charlie muttered.

"He knows."

"At least I didn't see *him* in this stupid place last night," Charlie noted, pointing to the comedy club facade, now shuttered.

Tucker laughed. "Too much for you, huh, old man? That girl was too much for you."

"You think that gal was funny?"

"Yeah. Damn funny. That bit where the guy who's trying to undress her gets a cramp was —"

Gravis interrupted. " As funny as a broken crutch."

"You just don't know what's happening, Charlie. That lady is what's going down. Stand-up comics letting it all hang out . . . going over the top. They make you think, old man. They take you apart and put you back together again. Anyway, you're always complaining about where I go and what I do. I go to see a band and you bad-mouth me. I go hear a singer, you bad-mouth me. I drink two beers and you rat on me to Tunney and the boss. Let's face it. I rub you the wrong way all the time."

It was an uncommon outburst. Charlie did not know how to respond to the younger man, particularly since his language was so weird. What did those things mean, anyway? *What's going down* and *over the top*.

Cassius turned his grease-streaked face toward Trent Tucker.

"Okay," he said, grinning. "Nothing too bad. Looks like a clogged fuel line. And you need new plugs."

"How much is it going to cost?" Trent asked.

Bottoms blew on his hands as he silently and thoughtfully began to evaluate the charges.

Trent stamped harder, waiting for the bad news.

Charlie Gravis, however, was miles away. He was thinking about Trent Tucker cracking up over a lousy lover's cramp. And he was thinking about all those people paying all that money to see and hear and laugh at "what was going down."

"You took your own sweet time getting here," Didi snapped when the two detectives finally pulled up beside her Jeep. They were in Denham Taylor's state trooper cruiser, unmarked but still menacing.

Brasco, who was driving, said, "You didn't say it was an emergency. We had to say goodbye to the media people. Poor Hillsbrook. It seems that the Fat Man really didn't interest them that much."

Didi wondered why the Hillsbrook detective was driving the state trooper's car. She pointed to the NBC van. "Well, they still seem interested to me."

"They'll be gone by tonight. What do you have for us?"

She exited the Jeep and walked quickly to the greenhouse, followed by the two men.

"Take a look at this," she said, pointing to the bottom of the glass.

They squatted down and looked closely.

"Something scratched the glass," Brasco said. "What about it?"

"No. Look closer," she retorted. She squatted beside them and ran her hand across the blemishes, slowly. "Don't you see? Those were made by a struggling animal. Maybe while it was being held. Maybe confined. It could have been a dog, a small one. Or possibly a squirrel."

Taylor stood then. "I don't get your point."

"That's what probably made the mother cat angry enough to scratch Buster," Didi explained. "Outside, something was clawing at the glass. It's an old hunter's trick. Tie live bait to something and let it scratch away, panicking the creature inside the den or the nest."

"And you think it was done with malice?" Taylor asked.

"I don't know."

Brasco also got to his feet. "If you got us here you had to think it was important."

Didi was silent for a moment. Then she said, "If you are investigating a homicide it might be important."

Taylor replied with a trace of mockery, "In other words, Dr. Nightingale, you think there were two killers and they worked as a team. One coated the cat's claws with venom, then signaled the one outside that Buster Purchase was about to go back into the greenhouse. Then the terrier, or whatever it was, started clawing. Then, boom! The cat strikes. The shock and the venom worked quickly on a very overweight man with a weak heart. Is that really what you're thinking, Dr. Nightingale?"

His tone of voice irritated her. "Look, I don't even know if there was what you call a homicide."

"Bingo!" Brasco said.

"What he means," Taylor added, "is that if you really think about it, there is no way in hell this can be a homicide. Maybe it was only pranksters. Maybe even rattlesnake cultists. There are a lot of strange people walking around Hillsbrook." He laughed. "Maybe it was space travelers. Maybe even a skinny weatherman who cast a voodoo spell on a fat weatherman. Who knows? But nothing that we found points to homicide."

"Anyway, thanks for thinking of us," Brasco said. "And give my best to Allie Voegler when you speak to him."

The two men headed for their car. Didi shrugged. She had thought they should know what she had found. If it didn't mean anything, so be it. If they had come to the conclusion that the death of Buster Purchase was not a homicide, so be it. Given their slant, it would have been useless to tell them what Samantha had told her. There was no way of proving her stories about harassment, and Didi gave little credence to them anyway. But here, at least, was something concrete; there were some kind of scratch marks on the bottom of the greenhouse and they were not random.

Mouth pursed, she stared at the marks for a few minutes more, then kicked the snow and slush back over them.

She certainly could use a mug of hot cocoa. As a matter of fact, she wanted that more than anything else on earth right then. It grew large in her brain . . . She could envision it . . . steaming hot and sweet . . . She could taste it.

She walked swiftly to the red Jeep and drove home with Patsy Cline playing on the car stereo.

But after she reached home and headed toward the kitchen, in the rear of the house, Mrs. Tunney intercepted her, pointing toward the separate entrance for the clinic.

"The clinic is closed today, Mrs. Tunney."

"That's what I told the lady. But she wouldn't listen."

"Who is it?"

"I don't know."

Didi walked into the clinic. A woman, short, thin, in her thirties, sat holding a kitten in a cardboard carton. Didi looked her over, confused. "I'm sure I know you," she said, "but I just can't think of your name."

The woman smiled. "I was at that party the other day. That's where we met. You vetted one of Buster's kittens for me."

Didi looked into the box. Yes, it was one of Buster's kittens.

"My name is Ella Baker. I'm staying in Hillsbrook for the year."

"Why only a year?"

"I'm on sabbatical. Finishing off a thesis on women Weathermen."

Didi laughed. "When *did* women start outnumbering men as weathermen? It surely seems to be the case now on television."

"No, you don't understand. Not that kind of weathermen. I'm talking about the radical group who went underground in the U.S. during the Vietnam War."

Didi felt a bit silly. Trying to hide her embarrassment, she picked up the kitten and brought it over to the examining table.

"I wanted one of the other kittens," Ella confessed. "The ones that really look like bobcats. But I didn't have the money to bid on them. Anyway, at least she has a bobcat tail. See?"

Didi looked at the black-tipped tail. "What's the problem with her?"

"She was okay the first day or so. Then she just stopped moving."

"Stopped moving? What does that mean?"

"Well, look at her. She stands stock still. Sometimes for a long period of time. Sometimes she won't even move for food."

Didi stepped back. Small animals were not really her forte. But a few months ago she had stayed with a friend in Manhattan, Ilona Baer, who was a top-notch small animal vet, and cats were her specialty.

What had Ilona recommended?

You must develop a gestalt of instant diagnosis, she had said. Sure, blood and urine and stool workups were important, but the secret was balance, coat, eyes.

Watch the cat *move*, she had told Didi. Look at how the cat stands, lays down. Feel the cat's coat. Study the cat's eyes.

Didi studied the kitten. Her balance seemed perfect. But that really meant nothing because, just as Ella had said, the kitten didn't move. Critical balance was a function of movement.

She picked the cat up with one hand and ran her free hand briskly through the coat. It, too, was fine: lush, springy, not dry.

She turned the kitten around to get a better look at the eyes, and as she did so the kitten gave a little yelp and lashed out with her right rear foot.

Didi flipped the kitten over. "Hold her!" she ordered Ella Baker. Then she started to examine the pad on that right rear foot. Embedded deep in the pad was a small staple, the kind used in miniature staplers.

Dr. Nightingale took a pair of tweezers from the cabinet and quickly, easily removed the offending object. Then she washed and disinfected the paw.

"Sometimes," Didi noted, "pain simply disables a young animal. You won't even hear cries. It will just stop moving. To a great extent responses to pain are learned. The younger you are, the less you know."

"Oh, you are wonderful!" Ella Baker exclaimed breathlessly, as if Didi had just performed a twelve-hour heart transplant operation. She stared at the tiny piece of metal. "The poor thing must have been wandering around on my desk and just stepped on it. My desk is a mess. You silly thing!" She picked up the cat and hugged it.

Didi smiled. This Ella seemed to be in the long tradition of academics who seek out Hillsbrook for peace and quiet. People like that were always just a little off-kilter.

"By the way, Doctor, her name is Bernadine."

"A mouthful," said Didi.

"How much do I owe you?"

"Leave your address. I'll send a bill."

Ella cocked her head and studied Didi, who

was a bit discomfited by the gaze of the other woman. She also noticed, for the first time, that this small woman who dressed like a lumberjack was wearing very thick prescription eyeglasses.

"I'm making a pork roast this evening," Ella announced. "A large one. Several people are going to help me consume it, at around seven tonight. Dr. Nightingale, I would like you to be one of them."

"Thank you. I don't know if I can make it."

"Don't you like pork roast?"

"Yes, I do."

"So why complicate matters? There is nothing further to say. Seven it is."

Ella wrote her address on the desk memo pad. Then she put the kitten back into the box and walked out.

Didi sat down behind her desk and stared at the address. It was in town; one of the large old rooming houses on Merchants Street that had been converted into either private dwellings or bed-and-breakfast inns.

She wondered what would have happened if the kitten's problem had been serious and indeed a whole series of workups, tests, and other procedures would have been necessary.

The fact was, she knew nothing of the special problems of hybrid cats. Were there any special problems? She hadn't a clue.

Her eyes roamed along the wall of bookshelves—half-random, half-focused, searching for something, but she didn't know what.

Yes. There was something! High up, the second shelf from the top.

Didi left the desk, stretched her arm up to the high shelf, and retrieved *The North American Bobcat* by Stanley L. Yarrow.

The moment she opened the book she remembered that it wasn't a veterinary text at all, merely a life history of the bobcat. It would be no help at all in the treatment of hybrid kittens.

But she did locate a section in the book that concerned itself with bobcat diseases.

She read brief descriptions of tularemia, rabies, and cat scratch fever. She glanced at several tables of the numbers and kinds of parasites found in the bobcat's gastrointestinal tract.

And she noted brief mention of various fleas and mites found on the bobcat.

Didi laughed when she read an excerpt from a 1949 thesis that proved fleas will remain on a dead bobcat for as long as five days after expiration.

The book became more familiar to her. She remembered that she had bought it and read it while still in high school—long before she even thought of vet school.

She began to leaf through the volume slowly, enjoying the many old photos of bobcats in the wild, even though a few of them were grisly—the book had been written before the trapping of such animals was considered a moral crime.

She paused at a perplexing drawing. Ah, she understood now. It was simply a graphic side-by-side reproduction of the bobcat's tail and that of the lynx, showing the differences between the two.

She read the caption: *The tail of the Canada lynx is always shorter than that of the bobcat, and always has a black tip. The tail of the bobcat is always tiped with white hairs.*

Now, why should that information make Didi hesitate as she was now doing? Oh, of course.

It meant that the father of Bernadine was a Canada lynx, not a bobcat.

Bernadine had a black-tipped tail and she was one of the kittens who more resembled the mother, a domestic cat. Didi thought back. Yes, they all had tails with black tips. All the kittens.

Well then, she decided, the daddy was a Canada lynx. That was that. After all, lynx and bobcats were closely related, but still different species.

She closed the book and replaced it on the shelf.

Something else was bothering her: that brief conversation in the diner with Buster Purchase.

He had stated, proudly, beyond any shadow of doubt, that he was breeding a Hillsbrook barn cat to a Michigan bobcat.

Why would he lie?

Allie Voegler did not like his new shrink. The man said little, just watched and listened. His name was Jordan Pease. He was very tall, very thin, and awfully young. At least he seemed very young. He also had a mannerism that Allie did not like at all: from time to time he would touch his glasses as if he were about to remove them, but then, at the last moment, he left them where they were.

"The way I see it," Allie said, "strangers are going to make the final decision as to whether I live or die."

"Die?" Dr. Pease asked gently. "Has anyone threatened you?"

"No. No . . . I mean, you know . . . symbolically," Allie mumbled. "I mean that someone, maybe you, is going to have to say Voegler is fit to return to duty. Or, no, Albert Voegler is a violent individual who will always be a loose cannon. That's what I'm saying. And I don't think it's fair to be judged by strangers."

Dr. Pease just nodded. Allie realized this was not a good conversational path to follow. He sat back in the black leather barrel chair. Pease was behind the desk. There was a couch nearby, pushed up against the wall. Allie would never use it. He preferred the chair. The fingers of each of his hands grasped the underside of the chair arms tightly, then he released the pressure, then tightened up again. Like an exercise to strengthen the forearms, he thought. Why doesn't this Pease ask what he wants to know about me? Why doesn't he suggest a line of conversation? Why this ridiculous song and dance routine?

Albert Voegler leaned forward suddenly and said, "I haven't really told you the whole truth about Dr. Deirdre Quinn Nightingale."

Pease raised his eyebrows.

"Sure," Allie went on, "I love her. I want to marry her. I hope when this mess is over, everything will just sort itself out. But what I'm saying is that it wasn't only my fault. I mean the breakup. She can be a difficult lady. She's not the all-American girl everyone in Hillsbrook thinks she is."

"All-American?" the doctor repeated, shifting his weight in his chair.

"You know what I mean. The whole town gushed over her when she came back to Hillsbrook to be a vet. Isn't she wonderful, they said. Look how she's taking over her mother's house and taking care of those idiots who live there. Look how kind and responsible she is. Look how she reveres the memory of her mother. Look how she's building a practice from scratch. Yeah, they all made a big fuss over her."

Dr. Pease smiled. "Those sound suspiciously like the actions of an all-American girl." He was teasing the big cop gently, who didn't really get it.

In response, Allie burst out: "Of course she's like that. All I'm saying here is that if you cross her, she can show a different side. And it's cruel, harsh, vengeful. Believe me, she goes for the jugular."

"You have firsthand experience of that?" Pease asked.

"I don't want to talk about that stuff now. But believe me, I've seen it. For example, if she has to put an animal down . . . maybe she spends three days and nights with it, nursing it, doing all kinds of things. She's playing Mother Teresa in the barn. But when she realizes the beast won't recover . . . when she figures that the pain is too much . . . she turns on a dime. She says nothing to nobody. She doesn't want to hear what the farmer has to say. She puts that animal down. Fast. Just— bang! Fast!"

He waited for an acknowledgment of the shrink's understanding, but there was none.

"And she has a secret life," Allie added.

"Aaah" was all Dr. Pease said. It was enough.

"There was only one man she ever loved, and believe me his name isn't Voegler. It was a professor of hers. He seduced her and then dumped her. This happened in Philadelphia, where she was going to vet school. She never got over him. She never will. I know it. She knows it. Her friends know it. One day she may marry me, but believe me, what she is always looking at is her broken goddamn heart. Do you understand what I'm saying?"

"Are you bitter?" the doctor asked.

Allie found the question so funny he burst into great rollicking laughs. And then the session was over.

Didi was wearing the black wool pants suit that Rose had talked her into buying last winter. As she rang the doorbell she wondered, once again, why she had neglected to take Rose with her on a social occasion. Ella Baker, no doubt, would have welcomed her.

The door was made of filigreed glass and Didi could clearly see even from outside on the doorstep that the party was in full swing. She immediately realized that this pork roast feast would be a capsule repeat of Buster Purchase's fatal bash.

She could see the Napiers, the Mintons, and Jeremy Lukens milling around inside. Then she caught sight of Ella Baker striding toward the door to let her in.

Didi smiled brightly. Maybe this was a post-adoption party, for it seemed that all the guests had bid on and purchased a hybrid kitten at Buster's soiree.

Hybrid *lynx*, she recalled. Not hybrid bobcat, as they all thought. Though of course if didn't really matter.

The door swung open and a beaming Ella Baker, wearing an elaborately beaded sweater, escorted her into the spacious parlor.

"And how is Bernadette?" Didi asked.

"Bernadine," Ella corrected her, "and she is fine."

Didi squirmed as Ella introduced her as Dr. Nightingale. Any introduction was superfluous. Didi—in her fashion—knew all the guests and they knew her. This was Hillsbrook.

Of course, she had never said more than five words to Trevor and Patricia Napier, but she knew the reputation of this elegant older couple. They were old money, Hillsbrook hunt people, but not at all snobbish. In fact they had a reputation for being reclusive, almost saintly pillars of the community—people who gave to charity, who supported everything that made

Hillsbrook (as the Chamber of Commerce called it) the jewel of Dutchess County.

And she knew the Mintons even better. She had an account in Louis Minton's bank, and Charlotte Minton had treated Mrs. Tunney when she was in general practice.

As for Jeremy Lukens . . . well, Mrs. Tunney had tried to get Lukens and Didi together; it was one of the old lady's many matchmaking fantasies because she was so unhappy about Didi and Allie Voegler.

This matchmaking didn't yield any results whatsoever, but Lukens had once dated Rose Vigdor. Rose thought the man pathetic, with his ambitions to make Hillsbrook the cultural hub of the county.

Didi sat down on a straight-back chair. Lukens brought her a glass of red wine. He was actually a handsome man, in his late thirties; a bit stout and a bit agitated, with thick black hair and a flamboyant mustache.

Charlotte Minton had obviously had one wine too many. She was chattering about Buster: "So I heard this lady in the post office talking to her friend. And she was saying 'Do you think the Fat Man is in heaven?'"

Charlotte burst out laughing. No one else seemed to find it funny. Charlotte pressed on.

"I wanted to tell her there was no doubt he is in heaven. Because he either died from rattler venom or from his bad heart, and everyone knows that both snake bite victims and heart attack victims automatically get their tickets punched upstairs."

Louis Minton clearly was becoming uncomfortable at his wife's rather fatuous comments.

Patricia Napier saved the moment by tactfully changing the subject. "What distresses me most," she said, "is what I heard when coming here tonight: that Sissy Purchase has left Hillsbrook for good. She just packed up everything and moved out. It's so sad."

Jeremy Lukens added, "People do strange things when they're grieving. It was all so sudden for her. And so brutal."

"Oh, come on, Jeremy!" Charlotte yelled boisterously. "The man had a coronary. I've seen lots more brutal deaths."

"It is that snake venom that gives the thing a brutal cast," Louis said.

"Yes, exactly," Jeremy said in agreement.

Napier expanded: "The notion that the snake venom was in the cat scratches and therefore on the cat's claws is quite unbelievable. It's incomprehensible. The thing makes no sense; not an ounce of logic in it. That is what makes it brutal . . . like a blue snowstorm."

"My husband has become a philosopher," said Charlotte, sarcastically.

Trevor Napier smiled at Didi. He looked like an eighteenth-century oil portrait suddenly come to life. "You know," he said, "when I was a young man, veterinarians were considered philosophers."

"That's exactly right," Ella burst in. "Old country novels always portray vets as kindly, philosophical rogues."

Lukens put his hand on Didi's shoulder, a bit too familiarly. "From what I hear, Dr. Nightingale has an exemplary personal life."

Everyone laughed. Didi shook off Jeremy's hand and finished her wine. Ella rushed into the kitchen, then called out, "The pork roast is ready!"

The guests all applauded her reentrance. She was carrying a tray laden with savory meat. As they filed into the dining room they began to chatter about their kittens. Didi felt warm and good.

* * *

"Put on the Comedy Channel, willya?" Charlie Gravis barked at the bartender. Charlie was in an ugly mood. His friend Ike Badian had refused to join him for a drink, giving that most lame of all excuses: a sick cow.

So there was old Charlie, alone, in this silly new pub on the main street. Sitting alone in the posh, leather-heavy, overpriced pub, like a tourist, drinking a small stein of dark beer—a brew with the word Oregon in its name. Oregon. Of all places. Oh well . . .

The only other customers were a couple down at the other end of the bar. He might have struck up a conversation with them, but they were lost in each other.

The bartender used the remote control to tune in the channel.

"Yeah," Charlie muttered to himself mockingly, suborning Trent Tucker's words, "I want to see what's going down now."

"There you go," the bartender said, with no enthusiasm whatsoever.

Charlie focused on the screen. The first comedian introduced was a short, hefty man with long hair who told jokes about Los Angeles. The audience was laughing hard but not a titter came from Charlie.

The second comic was a woman, tall, thin, blond, and oddly shaped, as if she had a curvature of the spine. She held the microphone tightly and spoke quickly in short punchy one-liners. Her routine was about working in an office with a sexually harassing "bozo." Charlie sank deeper into gloom.

Next came a black man in a funny hat. Charlie couldn't really understand the language used—slang, Charlie supposed—so he had no opinion about the humor or lack thereof in the act.

After this one, he turned away, stopped listening, drained his glass, and ordered another beer.

The TV droned on. Charlie surreptitiously began to watch the two lovers at the end of the bar. It gave him a kind of nostalgic glow.

"Hey, Pop!" the bartender called out.

"What?" Charlie answered aggressively, afraid the man had caught him peeking at the couple and thought he was a voyeur.

But that wasn't it. "If you want a laugh." the bartender said, "check this out. It's a *Saturday Night Live* rerun. An old one."

Charlie looked up at the screen.

It was a sketch in which John Belushi played his signature Samurai warrior character. This time he was working in a delicatessen.

A customer comes in and asks for a sandwich. Then all hell breaks loose as the lunatic Samurai turns on the cold cuts and begins constructing a sandwich.

Charlie watched bug-eyed. He had never seen anything like this in his life.

He began to laugh. Louder and louder. He lost control. He laughed until his stomach hurt and tears rolled down his cheeks and into his beer.

When the skit was over he yelled to the bartender: "Shut it off. I can't stand any more."

The bartender complied.

"Who was that chubby fella in the Japanese clothes with the sword?"

"Haven't you ever seen John Belushi?"

"No," Charlie admitted, wiping his face.

"A very funny man. Too bad about him. He died of a drug overdose. In a motel. A long time ago."

"How long?"

"Maybe fifteen years."

"Was he famous?"

"Are you kidding? The guy was a star."

"Then he made a lot of money?"

"A bundle."

Charlie didn't say a word for another ten minutes. He seemed to be lost in intense thought.

"Give me a whiskey, huh?" he finally said. "Make it rye."

"You sure you can handle it, Pop?"

"I think I can. I think my ship has come in."

The Mintons left first. Then the Napiers.

Ella, Didi, and Jeremy remained, sprawled on the sofa and the living room chairs, coffee cups almost empty.

Bernadine the kitten was playing with Jeremy's shoelaces.

On the low coffee table was a plate with the remains of an apple pie.

Didi was quite stuffed, quite happy. Recent events and traumas seemed to have been dissolved.

"It was the best meal I've had in a long time," she said.

"I'll second that," Jeremy added.

The hostess basked in their praise.

"Pariculary the candied yams," Didi noted.

"I thought they were sweet potatoes," Jeremy said.

"No, they were yams," Ella affirmed. "With a lot of honey and just a few cloves."

"People tell me," Lukens mused, "that yams and sweet potatoes are totally different species. I always found it difficult to believe."

Didi laughed. "Well, believe it. It's true."

Ella got up and put on a CD—an unidentified string quartet playing soothing melodies. Then she offered brandy, which Didi declined. Jeremy added just a dollop to his coffee.

"They are good people," Jeremy said softly.

"Who?" Ella asked.

"The Mintons. And the Napiers. And you and me. In fact, the whole damn town is good people. Sure, some are yams and some are sweet potatoes, but . . ."

He didn't finish the whimsical metaphor; he just let it hang there.

Didi closed her eyes and listened to the music. She wondered who had composed it. She remembered that earlier in the evening Ella had played exclusively jazz vocalists.

Ella, comfortable in her chair, said, "If it weren't for Buster Purchase's death, these past few months would have been the best time of my life. And maybe they still are."

Didi smiled, but kept her eyes closed.

Jeremy Lukens, perhaps a bit drunker than his two companions had realized, mumbled something about the nature of yams versus that of sweet potatoes.

We've all had just a little too much to drink, Didi thought, suppressing a giggle—and much too much to eat.

Suddenly Jeremy was on his feet. "I have to go," he announced. "Thanks for a lovely evening, Ella."

Didi opened her eyes then. Lukens forcefully shook hands with both women, then he walked toward the door. Ella helped him with his coat and saw him out.

"Can I help with the dishes?" Didi offered.

"No way. I'll do them in the morning."

"Well, the least I can do is help you clean up a bit," she said, and started to gather the empty cups and saucers before the other woman could protest.

Both Ella and Didi stopped in their tracks at the sudden burst of sharp noise from outside. Three rapid cracks had ripped through the air.

"What was that!" Ella demanded.

Didi still did not move. Nor did she answer. But she knew exactly what the noises were.

Ella, for some reason, ran over to the CD player, but she did not stop the music.

Then there was another sound. An even more terrifying one—a scream.

Didi flung the dishes onto the sofa and ran out of the house, Ella following her closely.

Jeremy Lukens was reeling, staggering back toward the house. His hands were outstretched.

Didi, after a moment's pause, rushed to him. His face was horribly contorted and blood frothed from his lips.

He fell heavily against her, his weight knocking her down. When she landed on the pavement, Lukens was on top of her.

It was only an instant before contact that she saw the bullet holes in his chest.

Lukens's blood was soaking her chic black outfit.

Chapter 4

Dr. Nightingale sat on the sofa in her blood-stained garment. Around her were the soiled dishes she had been bringing into the kitchen when she and Ella heard the shots.

It was a few minutes past midnight, the new day.

Didi had already called Mrs. Tunney and told her she would be sleeping at her friend Rose's place. The old lady was aghast, given the primitive quality of Rose's living quarters. Didi could not, however, bring herself to report what had transpired at Ella's—anyway, the radio would take care of that in the morning.

Rose, on the other hand, now knew the whole story. Didi had told her everything, and was most grateful when Rose said she'd be waiting up with hot tea and multiple blankets. That was good to hear; Didi needed a friend now.

The ambulance and the uniformed police had come and gone. The shock had worn off. All she felt was a great weariness, and the profound sense of being utterly alone.

Ella Baker was pacing the width and breadth of her home. In fact she had done little but pace since the murder. Detective Thomas Brasco had arrived around ten and had by now finished his interviews of the neighbors. Now he was seated on a low chair, notebook out, watching Ella as she paced ceaselessly.

"All we know," Brasco said, "is that he was shot three times, point-blank in the chest, at very close range. The weapon was a large-caliber handgun."

Neither Ella nor Didi responded.

"Had he been drinking?" Brasco inquired.

Ella shrugged.

"Was he drunk?"

She stopped pacing and fell onto a chair. She regarded the policeman with raw hatred. "Why would you ask such a question? What does it have to do with anything?"

"Do me a favor, Miss Baker," he said coldly. "Just answer the questions I put to you."

Ella fell silent. But she did not appear at all contrite.

Didi spoke up. "He wasn't really smashed," she said. "He had quite a bit of wine. We all did. And some brandy in his coffee. That's all."

"This kind of thing doesn't happen in Hillsbrook very often," Brasco said. "That's why I'm asking about the drinking. Maybe, just maybe, it fits into a drive-by scenario."

Ella's manner was still sharp and impatient. "I do not understand what you are talking about. This isn't L.A."

"Don't tell me where we are, Miss Baker. Maybe Lukens stumbled out of your place and onto the street instead of the sidewalk. Maybe a car full of crazy kids braked and swerved. Maybe they had words with him and he said something they didn't like. Somebody in the car could have been high on something, and just blew him away."

Dr. Nightingale grimaced. The "crazy kids" scenario. She'd heard that one before, from Allie Voegler. Why did cops cleave to that old saw so tenaciously?

Whenever no one knows what happened, it's always safe to look to the "crazy kids" explanation. And it usually came with the "drug-related" cliche.

Brasco flipped his notebook shut. But he continued to stare at Ella. "Does that make sense to you?"

She made a clucking noise. "Sure. Why not? But then again, maybe he was shot by that crazy old poet who wanders about town . . . or the one who runs the health food store. Maybe you ought to be looking for the Scarlet Pimpernel."

"You're in Hillsbrook to write a brook. Isn't that right, Miss Baker?"

"No. Not a book. A thesis."

"How's it coming?"

"Fine."

"Yeah, this town is a nice place to work in. Scenery. Lots of scenery. Quiet. A close-knit place where people don't stick their noses in other people's business. That's pretty rare. I hear in the fifties it was a regular writers' colony." Brasco paused there, laughing. "Dairy farmers and scribblers. A weird mix, huh? But then again, they both shovel manure, don't they?"

Ella sat in stony silence.

"It's too bad those TV people left town so quick," he said. "They would have had a real murder to babble about. But they were here for the Fat Man story—a celebrity. I don't think a small-town haberdasher would have interested them."

"Jeremy was a lot more than that," Ella snapped.

"So I hear. I guess you knew him better than most. Maybe a whole lot better."

"What is that supposed to mean?"

"It means, were you sleeping with him?"

Didi was astonished by Brasco's question. It had never even remotely occurred to her that Lukens and Ella might be lovers.

Ella's response was quiet and modulated: "The answer is no."

Brasco took that in, and then went on to ask, "Either of you know anyone who disliked Jeremy Lukens? Enough to put three bullets into him?"

Didi shook her head. Ella ignored the question completely, turning instead toward Didi and whispering, "What about Jeremy's kitten?"

"I'm sure it'll be taken care of," Didi answered.

"What are you talking about, Miss Baker?" the detective asked angrily.

"Buster Purchase's hybrid kittens. Jeremy took one of them."

"You mean one of those?" he said, pointing at Bernadine, who was now on the sofa licking the residue of milk from a saucer that still lay where Didi had flung it.

"Yes. One of *those*," she repeated acidly.

Didi was falling asleep. She fought it, but she was being pulled under. She had to get out of that house. The unhappy thought came to her that there was no hot shower waiting for her at Rose's—no shower at all. And she would have to borrow some of Rose's clothes.

Dimly, she could hear Detective Brasco ask, "Tell me then, Miss Baker, who *was* this Lukens sleeping with?"

Didi excused herself then, went into the kitchen, and, in an attempt to stay alert, threw water on her face.

But in another five minutes the interview was over and she was in the Jeep, heading toward Rose's barn. She was driving very, very slowly.

Abigail lay on her narrow bed under two blankets. Her eyes were wide open. She had been wakened, as she always was, by Charlie Gravis's big sow, Sara, who shared the barn with Dr. Nightingale's thoroughbred.

Sara's grunts were like an alarm clock; always going off at five-thirty in the morning.

The barn was at least a full hundred yards away from the house, but on cold mornings the grunts were particularly emphatic.

Abigail heard Mrs. Tunney walking down the hall from her bedroom to the bathroom.

She flicked on the small lamp, got out of bed, and dressed quickly. Then she made her bed, sat down on it, and waited for Mrs. Tunney to leave the communal bathroom and head for the kitchen, where she would begin the oatmeal.

It was cold in Abigail's room. She kept her arms folded for warmth and continuously wiggled her toes. As she sat there she found herself staring at the only chair in her room. It was a small, cane-back chair standing next to the door.

On the chair seat, in plain view, was a gaily wrapped package.

Abigail had no idea what it was or how it had gotten into her room. Had it been there before she went to sleep? She didn't know.

Quickly she retrieved the package and opened it on her bed.

What was inside made her catch her breath with excitement and joy.

Resting there was a small, black, spanking-new CD player—the kind one could either plug in to a wall outlet or use with batteries.

And along with it were three CDs: *Bessie Smith Sings, The Best of Joan Baez,* and *A Long Way Home,* featuring the pop-reggae contemporary singer Sister Carol.

There was a card enclosed: just a small stiff white card in an envelope.

On it was written in pencil: *Happy Birthday . . . Trent.*

Abigail didn't know what to do. She was so happy—and confused. Yes, tomorrow was her birthday. Yes, she had expected a small gift from everyone in the house.

But this? No!

How could Trent Tucker afford to buy such a gift for her?

She picked up the CD player, felt its weight, and admired its elegant design.

Well, she thought, what does it matter? He did give it to me. And she loved him for it. She sat there wondering how soon after breakfast she'd get the chance to plug in and play. Oh! There was so much to hear.

Mrs. Tunney was still in the bathroom. Abigail sat there and waited, happily reading the backs of the CDs.

Sara was grunting again. Abigail sent her a silent message that she would be fed soon. Abigail was always sending silent messages to the animals on the property—the pig, the horse, the barn cats, the yard dogs, and the deer that dug for shoots in the icy fields between the house and the pine forest.

Everyone laughed at her for sending these messages, but she didn't mind. After all, they couldn't hear Sara grunting in the morning either.

The sounds woke Didi. They were ugly, snarling sounds. She sat up, and for a moment she had no idea where she was.

Then she saw Rose a few feet from her, on a sleeping mat, sitting up also.

Didi spotted her soiled clothing near the now-cold woodstove. She was wearing a pair of Rose's jeans, which were much too big for her, and one of her sweatshirts.

"What are those crazy dogs doing out there?" asked Rose, rising laboriously as the barking and snarling became more ferocious. "Look! They pushed the barn door open."

"Maybe they were after a deer," Didi offered.

Both women hurried out into the frigid morning.

What they found was astonishing.

Burt Conyers was standing calmly about ten yards from the back of the barn.

Two of Rose's three dogs were in a frenzy, leaping and lashing at him, trying to rip his sheepskin vest from his body. The third dog was growling maniacally as he pulled tauntingly, cruelly, at the poet's staff-like cane.

"A beautiful morning!" the poet boomed out when he saw Rose and Didi approach. He seemed utterly indifferent to the assault.

The women attempted to pull the dogs off Conyers. It was not an easy task. All three animals were out of control now, barking and yapping more ferociously than before.

"Get the leashes, Didi!" Rose screamed. "I'll hold them."

Didi ran back into the barn, found the leashes, and a few minutes later the three panting animals were secured.

That accomplished, Rose then turned on Burt Conyers in a fury. "What the hell are you doing on this property?"

"My morning coffee," said the poet calmly.

"I didn't invite you for any coffee and you know it!"

"Yes, yes. But I prefer coffee with charming young women. Like yourselves. Late in life I have developed an intense affection for all of you. For your splendor, your bravery, your curvaceous . . . for all of your gifts."

"Get away from here now," Rose commanded.

Conyers shrugged, straightened his tattered vest, and with a tip of his imaginary hat strode off.

Rose and Didi were headed back to the barn, but they halted when they heard Conyers's voice boom: "Remember!"

When they turned around, Conyers was facing them with one arm thrust toward them, as if in warning.

"Remember what?" Rose asked contemptuously.

"As kingfishers catch fire, dragonflies draw flames." After a moment, he bowed and added, "Gerard Manley Hopkins."

The dogs began to yip crazily again.

Didi and Rose walked inside. Rose began to make coffee, muttering angrily, "I can't believe that idiot! Someone ought to commit him. I mean, doesn't Dutchess County have more asylums per capita than anyplace in the Northeast? Put that lunatic away!"

Didi folded the blankets she had used. "I'll bring these clothes back tomorrow."

"No rush."

When the coffee was ready, they sat facing each other, sipping from the large mugs.

"Are you okay, Nightingale? Feeling strong?"

"I'm fine. Thanks for putting me up."

"It's like a pajama party," Rose said, laughing, "except for Dr. Frankenstein showing up this morning. That fool didn't realize that my dogs weren't playing. They could have hurt him."

Rose shook her head. "Now that it's morning, Jeremy's murder doesn't seem real to me."

"Believe me, it was real," Didi said, pointing to her bloodstained suit.

"Want some breakfast? How about an egg?"

"No. I really have to get back now." Didi drained her cup, picked up the pants suit, and headed for the sliding doors, calling out as she walked: "I'll be in touch, Rose."

"You dropped something, Nightgown."

"I did? Where?"

"There. On the floor. It fell out of your pants."

She did see a small object on the floor. Of course there was no actual *floor* in Rose's barn—the dully gleaming object was lying on the ground.

Didi bent down and retrieved it.

"It's a key," she said.

"Car?"

"No."

"House key?"

"Not mine. Not anybody's, I don't think. Look at the shape of it. It looks like an old roller skate key. See, the end is hollow."

"Well, it's not mine," Rose said. "And I did see it fall out of your clothes."

Didi shook her head. She looked flustered.

"What's the matter?"

"Jeremy Lukens."

"What about him?"

"He staggered into me, Rose. After they shot him. As he was dying, he wrapped his arms around me. He knocked me down."

"And you think he put that key into your pocket before he died?"

"Yes."

"Oh, Didi. That's a bit of a stretch, honey."

"No. No, it isn't. That has to be the explanation."

Didi began to pace furiously, reminding herself of poor Ella Baker's furious pacing around her living room. Rose waited for her to slow to a stop.

"Did I tell you about the lynx?" Didi asked suddenly.

"What?"

"Listen to this, Rose. Buster Purchase lied to me. He didn't cross a domestic cat with a bobcat. He crossed a domestic cat with a lynx."

"So? What does that have to do with Jeremy getting killed? Or with the key?"

Dr. Nightingale didn't answer. She ceased pacing and picked up her empty coffee mug. She stared into it before she spoke. "Suddenly, Rose, I am very confused. And frightened."

"Why?"

She held the key up and rotated it in the sunlight filtering into the barn. "I have the funny feeling that Jeremy's murder had something to do with the Fat Man's death."

"Let me make some more coffee," was all Rose Vigdor could say.

Ike Badian was mucking out the barn to a bovine serenade when Charlie Gravis walked in.

"Thought you'd be on rounds," Ike said in greeting.

"The boss didn't get home last night. Trent Tucker dropped me off here."

"Grab a shovel."

"That'll be the day," Charlie replied.

Ike grunted and kept shoveling.

"Aren't you tired of all this?" Charlie said.

"No. I do it for the exercise."

"Put the damn shovel down, Ike. I got a proposition for you."

Ike did as Charlie asked. But he said, "I don't want to hear it."

"Now wait a minute, Ike. What if I can guarantee that in a few months you'll own and operate the biggest dairy spread in Dutchess County? Maybe even in the state? I'm talking about a big herd, fully mechanized barns, maybe even a bottling plant. I'm talking about a trained staff and an in-house vet."

"You're crazy, Charlie."

"And for me, well, first of all I'll get my boss one of those huge new equine hospitals . . . with a swimming pool . . . and—"

Ike picked up his shovel and began working again.

"Listen to me, will you?" Charlie urged.

Ike went on shoveling.

"Did you ever hear of John Belushi?"

"Who?"

"Belushi."

"I used to know a fella in the feed business name of Pat Belushi. He was from Hopewell Junction."

"No. This guy was a comedian."

"Oh. Don't know him then."

"He made millions."

"That's nice."

"Guess how?"

"He was funny?"

"Very funny. He put on one of these outfits, like a Samurai, and got himself a sword and a stooge and he just carried on like an idiot."

"Good for him."

"Let me tell you something, Ike. Comedy's what's happening now. Get it? Even Trent Tucker don't hang out in the sleazy bars any-more. He goes to comedy clubs. Him and all his friends. Get it? That's where the big money is today."

"What the hell are you trying to say, Charlie?"

"We're gonna be a comedy team."

"What?"

"Me and you. A comedy team. Not like Abbott and Costello. A dairy farmer and his cow."

"Hold on a minute, Charlie."

"We'll have them rolling in the aisles, Ike. Me as Belushi. You as the cow. Can you see it? First Hillsbrook. Then Vegas. Then Hollywood—TV, cable specials, everything. And that money will just keep rolling in . . . rolling . . . rolling . . . because people all over the world love farmers and they love cows. Do you see what I'm saying, Ike?"

"Calm down, Charlie. I'm seventy-four years old."

"That's right. A man your age shouldn't be mucking out a barn."

Chapter 5

Didi spotted Allie the moment she entered the donut shop on Route 28. Usually he waited for her at the window counter. This time he was at a table with a coffee and two untouched jelly donuts in front of him.

"You've lost some weight," she said as she slipped into the chair across the table from him.

"Not as much as Jeremy Lukens."

"So, you heard."

"Brasco called me early this morning."

"Any ideas?"

"You mean like who blew him away?"

"Yes."

"I'm suspended, Didi. I don't have ideas. I'm not allowed to have ideas. And if I do, I tell 'em to my shrink."

He laughed bitterly, then stretched his hand, palm up, across the table: She grasped it. "Damn, I miss you," he said. "Stay with me a day or so."

She pulled her hand back. "I can't."

"Okay, okay, sure. Let's eat donuts and talk about the weather."

His bitterness pained her. His need for her was obvious. His situation, she knew, was precarious. But she could offer him nothing—not love, not sex, not companionship. The wounds had not healed. It was as simple as that.

She pulled the paper plate containing one of the jelly donuts toward her.

"Can I get you some coffee?" he offered.

She shook her head.

"Water?"

"No."

"Eat it straight up then," he said, laughing.

"In a minute. Tell me, Allie, did you do any hunting this past fall?"

"Yeah. Didn't get anything though."

"Where did you go?"

"North and east. Up around the Connecticut border."

"Day trips or camping out?"

"Both."

"Did you see any lynx?"

"Lynx?"

"Yes. Canadian lynx."

"No, I didn't. I saw some tracks though."

"Are you sure it was lynx?"

"Not a hundred percent. But I hear they've moved pretty far down south now."

"It could have been bobcat sign," she noted.

"Hell, Didi, I know the difference between bobcat and lynx tracks. Lynx have bigger feet—big as a man's hand and covered with hair, like a snowshoe rabbit. Foot of a bobcat is like a domestic cat."

Didi took a small bite of the donut. Then she picked up Allie's coffee cup. She took a long swallow before she spoke again.

"Remember what you told me once? About how there used to be a lot of poachers working out of the Ridge?"

"Sure. In fact there were a *whole* lot of them at one time. Poached deer out of season and sold them to restaurants. Took beavers in the winter out of the state park. Trapped anything; sold anything."

"Do you think there are any left?" she asked.

"Maybe one or two. An old guy named Carey Bottoms. But why are you asking this stuff? What is this all about?"

"I'm just curious."

She took out the hollow key then and slid it across the table to him.

"What's this?"

"You tell me," said Didi.

He picked it up. "It's just a plain old key."

"Are you sure, Allie? I don't have any keys like that. Look at the hollow shaft."

"It's for an outdoor thing."

"I don't follow."

"Like one of those storage bins people put up on cars or in boats. You've seen them. The locks are set back deep to protect the mechanism from the elements. They make the keys long and hollow."

He handed the key back to her.

"First lynx . . . then poachers . . . then keys. Now what, Dr. Nightingale?"

"Donuts," she answered.

The two men sat in the truck—Ike behind the wheel and Charlie Gravis beside him. The truck was parked just off the road in front of a small battered frame house with a pink porch.

"All I know about the lady is that her name is Inez, she used to pick in the orchards, and now she sews up a storm."

"Charlie, look, maybe we're going about this the wrong way. Shouldn't we get some writers? Don't comedians have writers? I mean, how do we know this bit is going to be funny? Besides, we don't even know what we're going to do once we get up on the stage."

"Believe me, Ike, I know. It's all in my head. And it's funny. We can rehearse without the outfits. But we got to have them ready. And we don't need writers. We're doing what Belushi did. I think it's called rough pantomime, or something like that. It's boffo stuff. Funny, that joint is called the Three Stooges, but they're just being cute. The girl I saw onstage has nothing to do with the Three Stooges. We do. Boffo! A crazy Samurai is trying to milk a crazy cow."

"Okay. Okay."

They exited the vehicle and approached the house. Inez opened the door before they climbed the porch. "What do you want?" She looked fearful. Her hand clutched her neck. Inez Gramma was a short, stout woman with a part in the middle of her black hair and two long pigtails. It was obvious she did not want these strangers in her home.

"Ma'am, we need some clothes made," said Charlie.

"What kind of clothes?"

"Not a wedding dress."

"So? What?"

Charlie turned to Ike. "Where's the book?"

"You left it in the truck."

Charlie turned back to the vehicle and returned clutching an oversized library book. It was an illustrated history of Japanese cinema. He had marked the stills from the movie *Samurai II*.

"This!" Charlie said, climbing the steps and approaching the woman. Ike followed. Charlie showed her the photograph of Toshiro Mifune with his sword raised.

"*That's* what you want?" the seamstress asked.

"Yes. A Samurai robe and those funny-looking pants."

"So you don't want clothes. You want a costume."

"Right," Gravis answered, not really understanding the distinction.

"A costume is expensive."

"That's all right. We'll pay. But we also need something else."

"Go ahead. Talk."

"A cow."

"Who?"

"A dairy cow costume. You know. The whole thing. Something you can put on and suddenly you look like a cow."

"Hmmm . . . ears? Tail?"

"Yep. The whole cow."

"And the thing underneath?"

"Yep. The udders too. Most important. Got to have the udders."

Charlie was doing all the negotiating. Ike, looking steadfastly down at the ground, was too embarrassed to speak.

"So you need two costumes, right?"

"That's it."

"You have the fabric?"

"No. You get it."

"What kind?"

"Don't matter. Just one thing gotta be a Samurai, and the other a cow. It's just that simple."

The woman fell silent. She seemed to be evaluating the two old men.

"Well?" Charlie pressed. "How much?"

"Three hundred. I'll need a deposit of a hundred and fifty."

Gravis whistled softly. Ike merely groaned. Charlie gave Inez the library book. "Pay the lady!" he ordered Ike.

Detective Brasco stood smoking on the main street of Hillsbrook, just outside Harland Frick's natural food store. It was getting a bit warmer. Brasco intuited snow. He wished fervently that the state troopers had not pulled out when they decided that the Fat Man's death could not be construed as a homicide.

Just as he had intuited snow, he intuited a very difficult time with the Lukens homicide.

Odd, he thought, how fantastical Buster Purchase's death was, and how utterly, totally mundane the haberdasher's death was. Three bullets in the chest. Boom. Boom. Boom. Close range.

He finished the cigarette and walked inside. The old merchant Frick was unpacking jars of organic peanut butter. Harland laughed when he saw the detective enter and approach.

"What's so funny?" Brasco demanded.

"Nothing, really," said Harland. "I just

knew you'd be here. I figured everyone would think that I knew something secret about Jeremy Lukens. After all, don't I know a whole lot of things about Hillsbrook? And wasn't his store just down the block from mine? The trouble is, I don't think the man had secrets . . . and I don't think he was a secretive man. You understand? And if he was, I wouldn't know."

"That's a mouthful," Brasco noted dryly.

"In fact, Jeremy rarely said anything to me. He didn't like me much."

"Why was that?"

"Because I never bought tickets to those cultural events he was always tied up with."

"That doesn't mean anything. Few people did."

"He had been acting a little strange lately."

"How so?"

"Hard to say. He was walking around a lot on the street and it was pretty cold. Just walking up and down. Like he was agitated. No, wait . . . maybe not agitated, maybe happy. I don't know. But I would look up and see him through my window. He'd be walking one way, then back. Not dressed proper either. It didn't seem he was going anywhere; just walking like sometimes you do to relieve pressure. You know what I'm saying?"

"Not really. Did Lukens have a girlfriend?"

"Don't know. All I know about his social life is that he once dated Doc Nightingale's friend—Rose Vigdor. She told me about it, Rose did. She always buys here."

Frick was about to tell Officer Brasco about Rose Vigdor's passion for chips of all kinds. But it was plain that Brasco wasn't interested.

"Did he ever try to borrow money from you?" Brasco inquired.

"No."

Brasco picked up one of the peanut butter jars and studied the label. He asked, "Do you own a large-caliber handgun?"

"No."

"Tell me, did people like Jeremy Lukens, as a rule?"

"What people?"

"I mean people in the town. The other merchants. The shoppers. You know what I mean."

"Oh. Well, sure. Why not? Hell, look at me."

"What are you talking about, Harland?"

"I mean I'm a whole lot weirder than Lukens was, and doesn't everyone like me?"

"You said that Jeremy Lukens didn't like you. You said that just five minutes ago."

"Maybe my memory's bad. Funny, I can remember a small barn fire in Hillsbrook fifty years ago, but sometimes I can't remember in the afternoon where I was in the morning."

Fifteen minutes later Detective Thomas Brasco was seated on a folding camp stool in front of the wood-burning stove in Rose Vigdor's "remodeled" barn. The three dogs were circling him warily. He did not understand why Allie Voegler always spoke about this blond young woman with such distaste. Sure, she seemed a bit kooky, with all this nature-girl stuff. Sure, she appeared to be a hip city girl who had come to the country to save her soul, but so what?

"Am I going to be beaten during this interrogation?"

Brasco laughed. "Not with your dogs staring at me like that."

"Then I'll make you a cup of coffee—unless there are some kind of rules against fraternizing with suspects."

"I don't want any coffee. And you're not a suspect in this case."

"But you . . . know?"

"Know what?"

"That I dated Jeremy Lukens."

"Yes, I heard."

"Actually it was only one date. And that was almost a year ago. He liked me. I didn't like him."

"Why?"

"Look, I came here to get away from city culture. He seemed determined to import it."

He nodded. "Did you sleep with him?"

"No."

"Did he call you for another date?"

"Yes. But I refused to see him again."

"And did he keep pressing?"

"No."

"What did you do on the one date you had with him? What did you two talk about?"

Rose laughed and began pulling Bozo's tail, who emitted a mock howl. "Let's just say," Rose answered, "there was no dialogue with us. Just a monologue. You know men. They seem to think I'm just dying to hear their auto-biography. So he droned on and on about him-self. All I remember is that when he was a kid he wanted to be an artist . . . a painter . . . and he went to a few art schools and lived in L.A.

and New York and Rome. And then he came to Hillsbrook."

"That's it?"

"That's it."

The little Corgi, Huck, started to worry Brasco's shoelace.

"There was something odd about the guy," Brasco said. "He goes to dinner parties. He has a store in town. He's always getting up events like literary evenings, poetry readings, art shows, concerts by visiting pianists. And he's a Hillsbrook resident for many years now. But he doesn't seem to have made one friend. I mean one person who knew him well."

Rose considered what Brasco had said. "Yeah. Sad, isn't it?"

Ike Badian's pickup was in the Three Stooges parking lot.

"Place looks closed," Ike observed.

"You stay here," replied Charlie Gravis. "Let me handle things." But Charlie didn't get out of the truck immediately. "We need a name, Ike. A stage name."

"How about Mount Fuji and Eloise?"

"No. Something neutral." Charlie said impatiently. "Like Nichols and May. Or maybe the kind of a name a singing group would have. Short and sweet—like the Platters. I hear this Belushi guy made a movie a long time ago called *The Blues Brothers*. What about calling us the Moos Brothers? Or the Udder Brudders?"

"The *Udder* Brudders!"

"Don't work, huh? Well, all right. Look—you got a deck of cards?"

"In the glove compartment."

Charlie extracted the deck, shuffled it, and fanned the cards out on the seat between him and Ike. "Pick a card."

"Why?" Badian asked, suspicious.

"Shut up and pick, Ike."

Ike chose a card and turned it face-up. "Deuce of clubs," he announced.

"That's us," Charlie said. "We're gonna called ourselves the Deuce of Clubs."

With the name settled, Charlie strode into the Three Stooges Comedy Club and Bar. A young woman was mopping the stage. She was, Charlie realized, the same individual who had been the hostess on the night he'd picked up Trent Tucker . . . the same one who'd given him a hard time about the admission price. No, it was definitely not a good idea to talk to her about the debut of the Deuce of Clubs.

He spotted a young man reading a newspaper at the bar and walked over to him.

"I'm looking for the manager," Charlie announced.

The young man had a pleasant face. He was wearing a dark suit with a white dress shirt but no tie.

"I'm the manager, owner, booking agent, bouncer, and spiritual adviser," he said pleasantly.

"Good. I'm looking for work."

"What kind of work?"

"Comedy. Me and my partner. You ever hear of us—the Deuce of Clubs?"

"No. Where have you worked?"

"Oh . . . lots of places. A whole lot. You sure you never heard of us? We're the Deuce of Clubs."

The man gave Charlie a long, intense, analytical stare. Then he rose, walked behind the bar, dug up a flyer, and handed it to Charlie.

AMATEUR NIGHTS. OPEN MIKE.

WEDNESDAYS AND THURSDAYS. SIGN UP AT 9:30.

LET'S SEE IF YOU'RE FUNNY.

Charlie folded the sheet of paper and pocketed it. Gotta start somewhere, he told himself as he headed happily back to the truck.

The Ridge lay just north of the town of Hillsbrook, a series of jagged hillocks and ravines. It was populated by poor people. Their houses were ramshackle, often without running water or electricity. And the reputation of the populace was very bad indeed. Car theft was the major crime in Hillsbrook and it was believed that most of the stolen cars ended up in the Ridge, where they were chopped up for parts or repainted quickly and shipped to neighboring states for resale.

Doctor Nightingale parked her red Jeep halfway up the treacherous feeder road and walked the rest of the way. It had begun to snow lightly.

She felt light-headed, a bit foolish. She could not really justify her growing obsession with the lynx-bobcat problem. But she believed that it was crucial, that it went somehow to the heart of the matter. What matter? Two dead men.

Carey Bottoms's dwelling was pathetic; a patchwork of plywood over a sheet metal and brick frame. It looked like a smokehouse in a third-world country.

Attached to one side of the house was a long open shed under which stood stacks of cut firewood. In winter, many residents of the Ridge earned money by selling illegally cut firewood.

On the other side of the house stood the propane tanks and the portable generator—common features in the Ridge.

The door opened at the first knock. Didi found herself staring at a lean, cadaverous, extremely handsome middle-aged man with an ugly scar that ran down the right side of his face, from the hairline to the jawbone.

"Carey Bottoms?"

"Sometimes."

Didi laughed; she was a bit nervous. "I'm Deirdre Nightingale. I'm a vet."

"My dog's dead."

"I'm not here because of your dog, Mr. Bottoms. I'm here because of Buster Purchase."

"The Fat Man is dead too."

"Yes. I was there when he died, in fact. I vetted the kittens he was auctioning. They were hybrid kittens, he said. Domestic cat crossed with Michigan bobcat, is what he said."

"Why don't you get out of the cold, Doctor?"

Didi watched him carefully as he spoke. Was that a flicker of fear on his face? She couldn't tell for sure.

Didi walked inside. The inside of the place was a shambles—tools, clothes, chests. Two rifles were propped up against the wall in one corner. She felt a sense of excitement, perhaps dread. This was the first real-life poacher she had ever met.

Once inside, out of the wind and the cold, she realized that Carey Bottoms was much older than he looked; but his movements were vigorous, almost pantherlike. He wore an old army wool shirt with an insignia at the shoulder, thick corduroy pants with a rope for a belt, and construction boots.

He sat down on what appeared to be a keg, and waited, his face impassive.

"So you sell firewood, Mr. Bottoms."

"Yeah. You need some?"

"No."

"Too bad."

"I hear you also do some hunting and trapping," she said.

"In season."

"What about lynx?"

"You're in a dreamworld. No lynx around here. Used to be bobcat, but that was a long time ago."

"I've been told that Canada lynx are coming down, that they've been seen here."

"No lynx in Dutchess County."

"Are you sure?"

"Now that's a philosophical question, lady. A man like me don't answer those kind of questions."

Didi had a sense of déjà vu. Someone at the dinner party had talked about philosophical questions.

"Then I'll make it nonphilosophical," she said. "Did you trap a lynx for Buster Purchase?"

"I think this visit is over, Dr. Nightingale. I think you better walk right out of here and go back where you came from." He went over to the front door and opened it. "But look . . . no hard feelings. It's nice to get a visit from a pretty lady. And I'll tell you what I'm going to do. Two things. First, on the way out, pick yourself up an armful of wood. On the house. And second, if I see a lynx, I'll send you his tail."

Didi walked out, a bit angry, a bit frightened. But not angry or frightened enough to refuse the offer of free wood. She headed for the shed, picked up a few logs, and started walking toward the Jeep.

She stopped suddenly. Her eyes had caught a strange object behind the shed, on the ground, only half-sheltered by the overhead, but covered haphazardly by a tarpaulin.

It was one of those portable storage bins Allie Voegler had spoken about.

Didi looked quickly back at the house. The door was shut, windows too clouded to see through.

Was it possible? Was it plausible? Was it safe?

She crouched low and rushed to the bin, pulling the tarp off and exposing the lock. Then she dug into her jeans and retrieved the key.

It fit! *Click.* It opened!

She felt a rush of triumph. Opening the lid, she saw clothing, carefully folded. And in one corner of the bin there was a small duffel bag, knotted shut. Quickly her hands patted through the clothing. Nothing.

Then she picked up the duffel bag, thrust it

under her jacket, closed the bin, and headed for the Jeep, leaving the firewood on the ground.

Sweating and nervous, she started the engine and went too fast down the feeder road, skidding dangerously.

When she reached the main road, she gunned the engine, then drove out of the Ridge and onto the tarmac of the first gas station she saw.

Her hands were trembling as she shook out the contents of the duffel bag.

There were only three items. But they were astonishing—and inexplicable.

A thick rubber band was wrapped around seven or eight plastic sandwich Baggies. In each Baggie was a small clod of dirt. Along with a crisp hundred-dollar bill.

A small sketch pad with charcoal drawings of a woman who was half-animal. Each drawing was obviously of the same woman, but sometimes she was half-horse, sometimes half-cat, sometimes half-dog. A kind of shifting Lady Centaur.

A manila envelope in which were several bank statements from an Albany bank. The name on the statements was Save the Magruder Farm Committee. The balance in the account was $126,771.

Didi leaned back in the seat and closed her eyes. She didn't know whether to laugh, cry, or beep her horn.

Chapter 6

Ike Badian's house was a paean to domesticity gone to seed. Since his wife died, things just seemed to accumulate and spread. The only truly clear space was the kitchen, and it was there that Charlie began the rehearsal.

"Imagine," he said, "this is the stage of the Three Stooges Comedy Club. There, the refrigerator, is the audience. And your stupid old toaster is the mike."

Badian chomped down on his unlit cigar.

"I'm really getting a little nervous about all this, Charlie."

"Stage fright. Not to worry. I hear all good performers get it. Now, let's run through our bit. You go on first. You're in the cow costume. You look like a cow. Ike, you *are* a cow. You stand there. Moo a little. Then in comes a fierce Samurai, sword and all. He is startled. He doesn't know what the hell a cow is. He shouts in Japanese—Hai! And draws his weapon. He circles and threatens the cow. The cow looks unworried. Then he decides it's not an enemy. He sees the cow's udders. He looks close, perplexed. He pulls one. A little milk squirts out. He tastes it and is very happy. He decides to milk the cow. First he sits cross-legged and goes through a Samurai meditation. Then he lays his sword down, takes out his rice bowl, slips it under the udders, and starts to milk the cow. The cow kicks him off his feet. Grasping his sword, assuming the Samurai position, he threatens and circles the cow. The cow moos. The Samurai moos back . . . soon you gotta little singsong going . . . Oh, can you picture it, Ike? Can you see it? They'll be rolling in the aisles."

"You think so, do you?" Ike asked.

"Money in the bank."

"You don't talk Japanese, Charlie."

"Neither do Samurai. They just grunt and yell."

"What happens next?"

"He tries to milk her again. Gets kicked again. Tries again. The cow sits on him. And the final indignation is the cow pisses on his foot—you need to remember to keep a bottle of water with you, Ike—and then the Samurai commits suicide."

"And that's funny?"

"It's a whole new world out there, Ike. That's what's going down now. A little misery with the jokes. The kids love it."

"What if I forget my lines?"

"You got no lines. All you do is moo. And I'll guide you through the rest. Of course, I may improvise a bit. You know, Ike, I got a weird feeling that I may be one of those comic geniuses."

Ike started to say something. But Charlie cut him off. "Remember, old buddy: the talent may not be equal, but we split fifty-fifty on the money."

Didi walked slowly around the perimeter of the Magruder barn. Only the stone foundation was pristine; the frame had been replaced many times over the years. Now, even the last alteration, done some twenty years ago, was buttressed by nailed slats.

She peered inside through the slats. Not a large barn at all; maybe large enough for four cows and two horses and a few pigs. And probably a handyman or a relative of the owner sleeping there. In Hillsbrook in the eighteenth century, people shared space with animals.

No traces of the stalls remained within, but she could see stacks of old wood—pitted, cracked, warped. Obviously the renovators over the years had wisely preserved the original wood or what they perceived to be original.

If the barn ever achieved landmark status, Didi realized, it could be restored quite well.

She never understood why old barns had been built so small, so toy-like. Turning, she gazed around the Magruder property. An old well. A burnt-out house. One remaining hitching post. It was not a very pretty piece of land in any season. In winter, all there was to see were the tops of evergreen shrubs and a few naked rogue fruit trees.

Didi had not known that a really serious effort to preserve the barn had already started; she had no idea that a committee already existed and so much money had already been raised.

Had there been other hybrid kitten auctions? She didn't know of them. And she had no idea that Jeremy Lukens was the leading light behind the Save the Magruder Farm Committee. She thought it was the Fat Man. But if it really was Jeremy, why not be proud of it? Why hide the bank statements in a bin up on the Ridge?

She started back to the Jeep. She stopped suddenly. What if the items in that bin had not belonged to Jeremy? What if the key had reached her pocket through some other source . . . some other route? There had been other people at that dinner party.

No, not plausible. She looked around one more time. The county or perhaps the state owned the land now. The last Magruder to die had left no relatives at all and a whopping tax bill. To make matters worse, a few months after the death of the last Magruder the house had burned down.

It was even doubtful that, given the real estate depression in the Hillsbrook area, the land could be sold to a private developer. No one built in Hillsbrook anymore. And, to face facts, it didn't seem that spectacular an architectural or historical memento to earn it the coveted landmark status.

The whole thing was most peculiar. She scuffed the ground with her boot, like a horse looking for shoots beneath the snow. Then Didi laughed at herself as she pawed . . . at her inadequacy, at her perplexity; at her feeling that she was in the very center of the storm and yet she could not even tell which way the wind was blowing.

She went back to the Jeep and stared at the three objects she had found at Carey Bottoms's place. The small Baggies with the dirt and the hundred-dollar bills were still totally incomprehensible.

The erotic drawings were rather pretty, but they told her absolutely nothing.

Only that bank statement seemed real. It occurred to her that only a banker would be able to help her.

She drove into town to see the banker she knew: Louis Minton.

The moment she walked into his office his face turned pale and he stood up behind his desk.

"I'm sorry to barge in like this."

"Oh my, that's okay. It's so good to see you. Charlotte and I were worried. It must have been terrible. I heard you were there when Jeremy was shot. Right there. What a horrible ending for a beautiful dinner party. It's difficult to believe it happened in Hillsbrook. Sit down. Please, sit down."

She sat down on the chair across from him. He remained standing.

"I can't really believe it. Does anyone know anything? Do the police have a suspect?"

"I don't think so, Mr. Minton."

"Incredible. Absolutely incredible. The Fat Man's bizarre death was bad enough. But now . . . this."

"I need your help," Didi said.

"Of course. Whatever I can do."

"Just some answers."

"Answers to what?"

"The kitten you bid on at Buster's . . ."

"He's doing fine. Charlotte loves him to death."

"Did you pay for him then?"

"Yes. I had the check made out in advance. The moment I knew my winning bid I wrote the figure in."

"Who was the check made out to?"

"Mrs. Purchase—Sissy—told me to make it out to Buster."

"Why?"

"What do you mean?"

"I mean, why not make the check out to the Magruder Farm Committee?"

"Because the committee doesn't exist yet. That's what the kitten auction was for—to raise money to form the committee."

Didi handed him the bank statement. He stared at it in disbelief, then sat down. "Where did you get this?"

"That doesn't matter. I want you to confirm that the account exists—that it's real. And who opened it. There's no name on it. It's sent to a post office box."

Louis Minton nodded and kept studying the paper. "What I don't understand," she said, "is why Buster would run an auction like that when there's already this kind of money in the committee's account."

Didi added, "And why wouldn't he tell anyone that the committee was in existence?"

Minton nodded. Then he spun his Rolodex, found a number, and made a call to a bank in Albany. He asked for someone named Nolan. Minton read the number of the account off the statement and waited. Then he began to write, nodding as he took down the information. Then he thanked Nolan and hung up.

"Not Buster Purchase! It was Jeremy Lukens who opened the account. About six months ago. Isn't that strange!"

They sat together in silence for a long time. Finally Didi thanked him for his help and drove home.

Once at the house, she didn't go directly inside. She went to the barn with a large carrot to see her horse Promise Me.

He whinnied when he saw her and stuck his beautiful face over the stall barrier to butt her gently. He did it by swinging his head from side to side. Didi laughed and presented the carrot. He began to chomp on it.

The big horse, she realized, was putting on some weight; probably because she rarely rode him when there was snow on the ground—and she didn't like to turn him out alone because he always rolled. In fact, he was one of the few horses she ever knew that longed to roll about in cold slush.

"Did anyone ever tell you that you are a mental case?" she asked Promise Me in a stern tone.

"But I love him anyway," came a voice from the shadows.

Didi turned toward the speaker, startled. Abigail stepped into view.

"I gave him an apple this morning," she said. "He's always hungry."

Didi nodded and smiled. The horse made quick work of the carrot.

"Something wrong with him, Miss Quinn," Abigail said.

That name, *Miss Quinn*, set her teeth on edge. She wished her elves would call her Deirdre, Didi, Boss, Doc Nightingale, Hey you—whatever—anything—anything but her mother's maiden name.

"Something's the matter with Promise Me?" she asked.

"No," Abigail said, "Trent Tucker."

Didi stepped closer. Abby seemed very calm, as she always did. But there was a wildness in her eyes.

"Something bad," the young woman stammered.

"What are you talking about? I saw him this morning. He seemed fine."

Abigail gestured that Didi should follow her. They walked into the small tack room. There, Abigail pointed in the direction of a small trunk. Didi looked down at the objects on the trunk's lid: a portable CD player and three discs.

"He gave them to me for my birthday," the girl explained.

Oh dear, thought Didi. I forgot all about Abigail's birthday.

"Nice gift," Didi noted.

"I went to a store after he gave it to me. It cost a hundred and twenty-six dollars. Not counting the three CDs."

Didi felt a rush of fear. She realized what Abigail was getting at. Trent Tucker didn't have a dime to his name. Where had he gotten the money to pay for such a gift? She flung the end of the carrot onto the ground. Yet another problem. The last thing she needed. She was going broke. She was surrounded by corpses. How much more trouble could she take?

And this, she knew, could mean big trouble. Young men in Hillsbrook were always getting into difficulty—too much freedom and too few jobs. It was a potent mixture.

All she said was, "You did the right thing in telling me, Abigail. I'll take care of it."

She walked quickly to the house, through the front door, and down the long hallway leading to the kitchen.

She stopped in front of Trent Tucker's room. His door was shut. There was no answer when she knocked. She knocked again . . . more forcefully . . . Still no answer.

Didi turned the knob and went inside.

It was not what she expected. The room was neat. No clothes strewn about. On the small table by the bed were two athletic trophies. The bed was not made, but the linen seemed clean. There were stacks of hunting magazines on a chair, spilling over onto the floor, with a few paperback books. The small bookcase contained no books, only audio equipment. On the walls were reproductions of old military recruiting posters, including one from the French Foreign Legion.

The only serious piece of furniture in the room stood along one wall. It was a large chest of drawers. She remembered it had once belonged to her father.

Didi walked over and ran her hands lightly along the dark mahogany wood. On top of the chest was another pile of magazines. These were recently purchased, she could tell, and all automobile-related—*Car and Driver, Road and Track, Hot Rod, Classic Auto*, along with a few British publications.

Poor Trent, she thought. Always fantasizing about a sports car of his own, burning up the roads of Hillsbrook.

The top magazine had a marker. She flipped to the page. A report on the road test of the new Corvette. Didi smiled. She looked more closely at the marker. Her smile soon vanished.

He was using a rolled-up hundred-dollar bill to mark his place.

There were four other magazines with markers. Each one was the same: a hundred-dollar bill rolled lengthwise into a thin tube.

For the longest time, she was unable to move. Then, finally, she walked slowly out of the room, shut the door behind her, and went into the kitchen.

No one was around. Not Mrs. Tunney. Not Trent Tucker. Not Charlie. The house was empty.

She walked to the Jeep, shook out the contents of the duffel, and stared at the plastic Baggies filled with dirt and money.

Then she drove to her friend Rose Vigdor's place.

John Newbold—who owned the building that housed Jeremy Lukens's store, the Cove:

Fine Men's Apparel, as well as the two apartments above the store—opened the door and walked in.

Detective Thomas Brasco followed him in.

Newbold gestured with his hands, expansively. "You take a look. One of the nicest properties in town."

Brasco nodded. The interior of the store was small but tastefully done—like a magazine cover. Brasco had passed it a thousand times over the years, but the idea of going in as a customer had just never occurred to him. The clothes were too expensive and too "country gentleman." Five-hundred-dollar tweed sport jackets. Cashmere mufflers. Fisherman sweaters from the Aran Islands. Exotic berets. No, not for him at all.

"Is there an office?"

"No," Newbold said. "He had a desk over there."

Brasco walked to the small alcove which contained a desk and a single file cabinet. Everything was tidy, in order. Phone. Small PC. Bills. Rough layout for a mailing announcing the coming Spring Sale. Checkbook in one drawer. Letterhead and envelopes in another. Stapler. Scotch tape dispenser. Pens. Pencils.

Correspondence with manufacturers in the file cabinet.

"No pictures," Brasco noted.

"What?"

"I said, he doesn't have any photos on his desk."

"So?"

"Let me see his apartment."

Newbold secured the store and then led the detective upstairs.

"He kept telling me he was going to move," the landlord said as they climbed the stairs. "Kept saying he didn't like the idea of living over the store. But he never left."

The three-room apartment was, like the store below, stylishly furnished and spotlessly clean. Brasco had the sense that while Jeremy Lukens had obviously lived here, the place didn't seem lived *in*.

Only the walls were lively—even riotous. There were dozens of museum reproductions and prints hung with abandon: Dali, van Gogh, Warhol, Joseph Cornell, the English painter Bacon.

The bedroom was, unlike the living room, without furniture or wall decorations, except for a bed and a large drafting table with accompanying swivel chair.

On the table were very large sheafs of drawing paper and tin boxes of pastels.

Brasco sat down on the swivel chair and inspected Lukens's work. He almost blushed. The pastel drawings were intensely erotic—male and female figures in very blatant, swirling sexual poses. Dionysian.

"He was pretty good, wasn't he?" Newbold asked, staring at the drawings over Brasco's shoulder.

"Yeah. But notice they don't have faces."

Newbold laughed. "Who needs faces?"

Brasco shuffled the sheafs. "Someone told me Lukens had been acting peculiarly lately. Did you pick up on that?"

"No. Not really. But I didn't see him too often."

"He pay his rent on time?"

"Always."

"Both places? The store and the apartment."

"He paid on the dot."

"Did he gamble?"

"Not to my knowledge."

"Drink a lot?"

"Rarely saw him take a drink."

Detective Brasco stood up and walked to the small bedroom closet. Suits. Jackets. Pants. A few shirts. All hung carefully on thick wooden hangers. On top, hats. On the floor, shoes.

Stuck in one corner were more large rolled sheafs of drawing paper. He opened them. Pastels again. This time landscapes. Still a bit surreal and flamboyant, but definitely landscapes. Probably the Hillsbrook area.

He shut the closet and walked back to the table. He stared once again at the erotic drawings.

"Isn't it funny," he mused out loud, "that the figures have no faces but they're all wearing clothing of some sort? The man drew sex fantasies but the partners are never totally naked."

"Makes sense to me," Newbold said. "Hell, the man was a haberdasher, wasn't he?"

It was a strange sight. Two young women and three dogs in a huge, partially renovated barn staring at seven little plastic bags on the ground—each one filled with a small clod of dirt and a crisp hundred-dollar bill.

"I don't know why you're so sure the bills in Trent Tucker's room and those bills in the Baggies have anything to do with each other," Rose said. Then she added quickly, "Other than that they're both hundreds."

"I can't give you a rational reason right now. But I know it. Do you understand, Rose? I know it here—deep in my stomach. Like sometimes you fix on the correct diagnosis even though the symptoms are just not there."

Rose touched one of the bags with the toe of her shoe, as if it were dangerous. Aretha picked one up in her teeth. She was gentle with it, as if it were a puppy. Rose swatted the shepherd's nose, equally gently, and Aretha dropped the bag.

"Do you think Trent got his money in a criminal endeavor?" she asked Didi.

"To be honest, yes."

"But he's never done anything wrong before—has he?"

"Hard to say. Sometimes he's just a bit wild. Sometimes he hangs with a bad crowd."

"At least he's imaginative," Rose said cheerfully.

"What do you mean by that?"

"Well, he hid the money in plain sight, didn't he? He used the bills like bookmarks in those magazines. Just rolled up. It's something like Poe's 'Purloined Letter,' where the letter was more or less right out in the open and thus not found at first because people were looking for something hidden."

"Not *that* imaginative, Rose. I found them rather quickly. Even though I wasn't looking for them."

Rose pointed to the Baggies. "And you think these are criminal too?"

"Of course." Didi grinned. "Unless they're some kind of art. Unless Jeremy Lukens was assembling a kind of avant-garde art show titled 'Baggies with Dirt and Money.' He was an artist, right?"

"So he told me," Rose said.

"Maybe he just planned to staple them up in an art gallery. On a bare wall . . . wait . . . I have a better title for the show. How about 'Seven Baggies in Search of a Home'?"

"You don't really believe that, Nightingale."

"No. No, I don't. Like Trent Tucker always says: I'm spinning my wheels. But I believe they are criminal objects. I believe Trent is involved. I believe . . ."

She stopped mid-sentence, crouched down, and picked up one of the bags, staring at it. "Could they be signs?"

"Signs of what? For what?"

"Some kind of code."

"You mean like a message?"

"Yes. A message, from Lukens to someone. Or vice versa."

"About what?"

"That I don't know."

"They could also be payoffs. Or gifts," Rose suggested.

Suddenly Didi began to stack the bags, almost feverishly. "The more I look at them, the more convinced I am they're signs. They're messages saying 'Do this.' 'Do that.' They're too much alike to mean anything else. You know how traffic signs, for example, have to be universal—uniform. That's what the contents of these Baggies are like. Uniform. Absolutely uniform."

"Didi, you are becoming, as an old boss of mine used to say, intensely speculative."

"Maybe. But I think we ought to just send these messages out . . . as is."

"Okay. But to who?"

Dr. Nightingale straightened up and smiled. "To Trent Tucker, for one. And to everyone who purchased a hybrid kitten from the Fat Man."

"You won't let go of your belief that it's all one ball of wax, will you?"

"No."

"All right. But listen. Say we distribute the Baggies. Then what? Since we don't know what they mean—if in fact they are mes-sages—we won't know what to look for when this 'someone' or 'someones' respond to the message."

"Surveillance, Rose."

"Are you crazy!"

"No, no, hear me out. Tomorrow we deliver these packets, anonymously, to the Napiers, the Mintons, Ella Baker, and Trent Tucker. Just slip them into their cars somehow. Then we watch and wait."

"That's a lot of people, Didi. There're only two of us."

"I'll watch Trent. You watch Charlotte Min-ton. We'll hold off on the rest for the time being."

"Why Mrs. Minton?"

"I have my suspicions about her. I don't trust her. She's too damn ubiquitous. Remem-ber: she adopted a kitten. *And* she was at the dinner party, *and* left before Jeremy was shot.

And she was the one who gathered the snake venom from the Fat Man's wounds."

Rose did not reply.

"Well?" Didi pressed. "Are you with me on this?"

"Sure, Nightingale. But why do I have the sense that this is the wildest wild goose chase you and I have ever embarked on?"

"O ye of little faith," retorted Didi scornfully. Then she scooped up the precious Baggies.

Albert Voegler did not like late afternoon sessions with his shrink.

But, for some odd reason, he was beginning to like this Jordan Pease. The man looked like a vulture on a limb, and Allie had always had a soft spot in his heart for vultures. He admired them. They were so damn fastidious, even if they were carrion eaters.

Allie sat down, taking his usual position in the barrel chair. He and Dr. Pease greeted each other as usual, with nods. Sometimes Allie would sit there for a long time without saying a word. But at this session he started speaking immediately, not only because of his new affection for Dr. Pease, the therapeutic vulture.

"We met the other day."

"You mean Deirdre Nightingale?" asked the doctor.

"Right. In that stupid donut shop on Route Twenty-eight. I couldn't be cool. I asked her to stay with me. I wanted to make love to her. Oh, I wasn't that explicit. But she knew what I wanted."

He looked up at Dr. Pease, a bit winded; the words had just tumbled out. He waited for a response from Pease. There was none.

Allie continued: "And she wanted no part of me. We were holding hands across the table. Like kids. And the minute I told her what I wanted, she pulled her hand away."

There was a long silence.

"You know what she wanted to talk about?"

"What?"

"Lynx."

"What links? I don't understand."

Allie laughed derisively.

"L-Y-N-X. You know. Like a bobcat. Only it's not a bobcat. It's a lynx. Can you imagine it? I wait for those visits in that lousy donut place to spend a few minutes with her, and she wants to grill me about *Canada lynx*. Have I seen any? Have I seen any tracks? Do I know the difference between a lynx and a bobcat? Stuff like that."

Again they were both silent. Allie began to twist in his seat.

"I've been thinking," he continued a minute later, in a calmer voice. "Thinking about a really strange possibility. Something I read about years ago. About a husband who caught his wife's mental illness."

"What does that mean—'caught' her mental illness?"

"Yeah. Like a cold. The wife started throwing furniture out the window in the morning and then in the evening she would bring the pieces back in. Pretty soon the husband started doing the same thing."

"Are you sure you aren't thinking about a *folie à deux*?"

"Yes . . . Yes! That's it."

"It has nothing to do with contagion—like T.B. The sane partner simply begins to mimic the behavior of the deranged one. But it is unconscious."

"It doesn't matter how you put it. That's what it is. Now, just follow me for a minute here, Doc. Listen. There's no way I wasn't around the bend when I started smacking that witness around. No doubt about it, I was nuts to do such a thing. But remember . . . at the time, Didi and I were about to get married. At least, we were close to setting a date. We were in love. I was, anyway. And we were sleeping together.

"Now, just keep following me. At that time, she was the sanest lady in the world, I'd say. But subsequently I've realized she may have been a bit off-kilter then. Let's face it. The lady comes up with these obsessions: bobcats. Lynx. Keys. Maybe—and I'm not positive about this—but maybe she was a bit crazy even then. And I kind of caught it. A quiet case of *folie à deuce.*"

"*Deux,*" the therapist corrected.

"Whatever. Do you understand what I'm saying though?"

"Clearly."

Allie felt suddenly very good. "That would explain a lot," he noted.

Chapter 7

The moment Didi finished her morning yoga exercise, she circled the house and dropped one Baggie onto the front seat of Trent Tucker's pickup.

Then she drove into town to place one in Ella Baker's vehicle. Rose would handle the Minton and Napier placements.

The problem was, Didi hadn't the slightest clue as to which car on the block belonged to Ella.

Finally, she walked right up to Ella's front door and fastened the bag there, by tying it around the doorknob, as if it were a soap sample.

Then she sped back home to keep an eye on Trent Tucker. This would be the easy assignment, of course. The young man had been given the task, by Mrs. Tunney, of shoveling a larger path between the house and the barn, and then around the barn.

Didi had no calls to return, no rounds to make, so she spent her surveillance time upstairs in her room, where she had a clear view of Trent as he went about his work.

She wrote letters, sewed on missing buttons, sorted laundry, cleaned out papers, paid what bills she could, and felt just a bit idiotic dashing from time to time to the window to make sure her suspect was still in view. She wondered how Rose was faring with the hyperactive Charlotte Minton.

Early in the afternoon she walked quickly past the pickup and peered inside. The Baggie was gone from the front seat. The message, if that was what it was, had been delivered.

At seven o'clock that evening, after the communal dinner, she heard harsh words being exchanged between Trent and Mrs. Tunney.

Didi knew this was the nightly preliminary to young Trent's stormy departure from the house. Mrs. Tunney always warned him loudly against drunkenness, fornication, fast driving, tardiness, and whatever else came into her head.

Didi heard the engine of the pickup truck turn over and idle. The moment she heard the gears shifting, she ran quickly to her Jeep and took off after him.

The road was dark. The wind was fierce. He was going more slowly than usual and Didi could not yet get a drift of where he was heading.

The absurdity of the situation slowly began to grow in her; she was following one of her own elves because she really didn't have the slightest knowledge about young Trent's life, loves, problems—anything. I may be an excellent practitioner of veterinary medicine, she thought, but my credentials as a boss are pathetic.

He began to slow down even more. Didi had to drop far back so as not to be seen.

Finally, to her utter astonishment, he pulled off the road at the Magruder property and drove right up to the barn.

Didi switched her lights off and idled by the roadside. She watched Tucker's movements. The only thing in her head now was the stupid refrain: What is going on? What is going on?

The lights were still on in Trent's pickup, the motor still running.

She dug into the glove compartment and found a small pair of binoculars. Just as she trained them on the truck, Trent shut off his lights and motor, exited the vehicle, and walked to the back. He took a shovel and three burlap bags out of the bed of the truck.

Then he walked past the barn and over to the burnt-out husk of a house.

She kept her binoculars trained on him.

Trent reached the back of the foundation and then . . . he just vanished from sight!

Didi swung her binoculars wildly from side to side in an effort to locate him. But Trent Tucker was not there. He had vanished.

Was he practicing magic? Was he a wizard? What had become of him?

She wiped her eyes and focused the glasses again, carefully going over every inch of the terrain. There must be a root cellar, Didi thought. All these old houses had one. Surely he's gone down there.

She sat and waited. It was growing colder. She turned up the heat. The minutes passed. An hour. She even dozed off for a minute or two. Didi climbed out of the Jeep and walked around in the chilly air to clear her head. She went back inside the vehicle and another hour crawled by.

Where in hell was Trent Tucker?

The moon finally was visible, peeking shyly through the clouds.

Then she saw him, literally rising up from the ground like a mushroom. Over one shoulder he was carrying a lifeless burden in a sack.

Trent dropped the thing heavily on the ground and then vanished again. When he reappeared he was carrying another burlap sack. Once again he deposited it on the ground and then disappeared from view. At last he stopped the fetch-and-disappear routine and just stood over the bags.

Didi refocused the binoculars carefully. He seemed worn out. He was breathing heavily in the frozen mist.

Suddenly there was a flash of light from the barn area.

Then Didi heard a sharp crack—three of them.

God! Someone was shooting at Trent.

She slammed the Jeep into gear and accelerated off the road and toward the barn. A figure appeared in the headlights, running toward the road. The figure fell, almost under the Jeep's wheels.

Didi slammed on the brakes. The Jeep skidded to a stop. She leaped from the vehicle, holding the binoculars by the straps like a weapon.

Now the figure was crouched and breathing convulsively . . . or weeping.

A pistol lay on the ground. Didi picked it up by the barrel and flung it as far as she could. Then she lashed out with her foot and sent the figure sprawling. The creature rolled over and lay still, face-up.

Didi stared uncomprehendingly at Patricia Napier. Dressed in black cap, black hooded sweatshirt, and sweatpants.

The thin mature face was as genteel and pretty as ever.

Didi turned and ran back to the Jeep. Using the car phone she dialed 911, requesting emergency medical and police help. Then she hurried to Trent Tucker, her chest heavy with fear, her whole body shaking.

Trent Tucker was giggling. "Look! Look!" he kept muttering in wonderment. Didi stared at the shovel on the ground. The bullets had splintered the shovel's wooden handle into dozens of jagged pieces.

She fought to catch her breath.

"Trent! What are you *doing* here?" she choked out in a fury.

"Digging."

"For what?"

"For dirt. What do you think is in these sacks? Diamonds? Potatoes?" He burst out laughing again.

He's in shock, Didi thought. "Trent, listen to me. Why are you digging here? What is going on?"

He reached into his pocket and brought out a Baggie. "When I get one of these, I come here to dig."

"Who sends them to you?"

"I got no idea."

"I don't believe you, Trent."

He sat down on one of the burlap bags. "I'm not lying. I only saw her once. A short lady with real thick glasses."

Didi stiffened. "Okay, Trent. Just stay where you are. Sit still."

She walked back to Patricia Napier. The older woman was still lying on the ground. She was mumbling, her eyes wide open.

Didi knelt beside her. "Why did you try to kill him? What did he do to you?"

She didn't answer.

"Did you kill Jeremy Lukens?"

Again Patricia Napier didn't answer. She seemed to be singing something. Didi couldn't be sure. It sounded like one of those obscure verses from the "Battle Hymn of the Republic."

Didi covered the woman with her parka and waited for help.

Ella Baker stared out her front window onto the bucolic night street. The wind came in gusts, like organ chords. The snow was intermittent; it was hard to tell whether it was fresh falling or blown about from drifts.

It was odd how silent the village became at night. No one seemed to venture out on foot or by vehicle. But of course, she realized, they were out there. There were restaurants and movies and shops that stayed opened late. There were bars.

She shook her head. Ella loathed the place and the weather. She could never get used to the cold.

Turning away from the window, she

watched the kitten Bernadine explore the two open valises on the floor, both half-packed.

Then she looked at the plastic Baggie on the end table, next to the telephone.

She bit her lower lip, thinking, then swiftly walked to the table, picked up the Baggie with the clump of dirt and the hundred-dollar bill in it. She took the bag into the kitchen.

There, she wrapped it in a sheet of newspaper, placed it into the sink, lit a wooden match, and set it on fire.

When the object was burnt to a charred crisp, she walked back into the living room and finished her packing. She seemed to be moving at a quicker and quicker pace . . . almost feverish in her actions.

Then she sat down and wrote a note to her neighbor Mrs. Radosh.

Dear Mrs. Radosh—My name is
Bernadine. Ella Baker used to take care of
me. But she was called away suddenly.
Please take me to Dr. Deirdre Nightingale
when you get a chance. That is where I
wish to live.
Thank you,
Bernadine the kitten

Ella pulled a large carton out of the closet. She taped the note to the carton. She punched breathing holes through the top flap. She lined the inside with wool sweaters. She placed small food and water dishes in one corner of the box.

Then she picked up Bernadine and kissed her.

"Now you listen to me. You'll have a good home with that vet. And you'll be outside now only for an hour or two. Mr. Radosh always gets home between ten and midnight. I lined the box. You won't be cold. And there's some goodies."

She kissed the kitten again.

"Will you miss me?"

She put the kitten into the carton and closed the top. Then she carried it and the two valises to the door.

Ella stood there and looked around. What had she forgotten? Nothing important, hopefully.

She opened the door and peered outside. No one around.

First she carried the packed valises, one by one, to her old station wagon.

Then she carried the box to the house next

door and left it, clearly visible on the front porch, halfway between the top step and the Radosh door. She said nothing further to the kitten inside.

She walked quickly to her vehicle. Just as she was opening the car door, she heard Mrs. Radosh's front door open.

This was the worst possible scenario. She didn't want to be caught leaving the kitten. She didn't want to talk to anyone. She didn't want to be seen running away.

Ella Baker slid quickly onto the front seat, slammed the door shut, jammed the key into the ignition, started the engine, wrestled the wheel, and kicked down on the accelerator all the way.

The station wagon shot out of the parking space. It started to skid. Ella screamed and fought the wheel. The car careened crazily for about thirty yards, smashing into the sides of other vehicles on the street.

It hit a telephone pole at the end of the street. Ella's head crashed heavily through the window on the driver's side.

"This is ridiculous," Ike muttered as he watched Charlie pull the costumes out of the pickup truck. "I mean, I thought they're supposed to have dressing rooms," Ike continued. "Who ever heard of getting dressed in a parking lot?"

"Cheer up. When we play Vegas, they'll give us suites for dressing rooms, with whiskey and crackers and anchovies, and showgirls with feathers."

Then Charlie handed him the cow outfit. Out of modesty, they both moved to the far side of the truck, out of sight, to dress.

"I see Jack Randolph's truck here," Charlie said as he maneuvered the Samurai costume.

"Yeah, I told a lot of the old guys. I figured it'll help. I mean, let's face it, Charlie. We may need old dairy farmers in the audience."

"Check out my Samurai sword," Charlie said, displaying the blade.

"It's a beauty. Where'd you get it?"

"From a pawnshop in Peekskill. Years ago. World War Two Japanese officer's sword."

"Just watch out where you swing it."

They both started breathing heavily in the cold night as they completed the last-minute adjustments to their costumes.

"Damn, Ike, not only do you look like a cow . . . you *are* a cow." Charlie looked on in admiration of the bovine figure. The costume was brown and white with red udders and floppy red horns. The tail was black with a red tuft.

"It's hard to breathe in here," noted Ike the cow.

"Don't button it all the way up. And remember, you walk upright until you get onstage. Then get down on all fours like a proper cow and give out a low long moo. Make it musical."

Charlie was now fully dressed in his Samurai persona.

"*Hai!*" he yelled in the guttural Samurai fashion. He brandished his sword. The wind dulled the shout.

A noise came from the cow.

"What was that you said, Ike?"

More mumbling. Charlie didn't bother to ask Ike to repeat his words. It was freezing. He kept his eyes on the side door of the club.

"This is for all the marbles, Ike. We're going to lay them out in the aisles. The Deuce of Clubs is going to take off! Zoom! To the moon, Ike!"

The old farmer stuck his head out of the outfit. "I feel like an idiot."

"You're an artiste. Do you have the bottle of water?"

"Yeah. Listen, Charlie. Don't you think we should have rehearsed more? I mean, gone over the lines."

"Lines? What lines? I'm screaming in Japanese. You're mooing. We don't need lines. Did Belushi have lines?"

The side door opened. A hand beckoned them in.

"Okay, Ike. Now, remember. You go on stage first. I lay back in the shadows. Then I amble up."

"Got ya."

"They walked through the side door. They could hear the announcer call out: "And now, ladies and gentlemen, the new comedy team, direct from the barns of Hillsbrook in beautiful Dutchess County—the Deuce of Clubs."

The cow marched onstage to wild, inebriated applause. The cow assumed a cow's position and let out a long, low moo.

The audience went silent.

A resplendent Samurai marched onto the stage.

Someone from the audience yelled out: "Is that really you, Charlie?"

The Samurai spotted the beast. He barked. He circled the strange creature with sword raised. The cow mooed and groaned. The Samurai challenged him to a fight. The cow flopped over.

"Run that crazy cow through!" came the call from the audience.

"Skewer that thing!" screamed another.

The Samurai touched the cow's udder. He noticed a liquid on his hand. He tasted the milk. He looked around and smiled.

The Samurai put down the sword, smiling. The cow stood up. The Samurai began to milk the cow.

Another rude voice called from the audience: "Hell! An old geezer like you can't do no milkin'."

And then a bucketful of milk was flung from somewhere out in the dark, drenching both cow and Samurai.

An enraged Ike Badian unzipped his costume and flung the pail back into the crowd. Charlie dropped his sword with a clang and kicked the microphone down into the table area. Then all hell broke loose.

Dr. Nightingale sat in the cold night air on a dirt-filled burlap bag. Next to her, on another bag, sat Trent Tucker.

They watched Detective Thomas Brasco bundle Patricia Napier into a police car. Then he wrapped the weapon she had used in a plastic bag and handed it to a uniformed policeman in the front seat of the car. The EMS people had long since left the scene.

Brasco walked over to where they were sitting. "There's a good chance that weapon was the one that killed Lukens."

Didi's response was terse—and angry: "You took your time getting here."

Brasco bent down and inspected the shattered shovel handle. Then he chuckled. "Things are really popping in Hillsbrook. We got a riot over at that new comedy club. And your friend smashed up a block full of cars and a telephone pole."

"What!" Didi sprang off of the bag in a panic. "Who? What friend?"

"Ella Baker."

"Oh . . . Is she okay?"

"Seems to be. She's in the hospital."

He was staring at Trent Tucker, but he continued speaking to Didi.

"That Napier woman wouldn't say a word. Did you get anything out of her?"

"No. She looks in pretty bad shape."

"Not as bad as *he* would look if Napier's aim had been better this time." He circled Trent. "So it's time we figure out what happened here, isn't it, Mr. Tucker? That's your name, isn't it? And you work for Dr. Nightingale. Don't you?" He laughed sardonically. "Maybe we all work for Dr. Nightingale. So, kid . . . what the hell were you doing here? What's the story?"

Didi stood over the still-seated young man. "It's time, Trent," she said forcefully.

Tucker looked first at Didi and then at Brasco, and finally said, "You want to go down, I'll take you down. But it ain't pretty."

"Do we need a beam?" Brasco asked.

"I got one. I work with it," Trent said. He then produced a huge flashlight.

"Tell him!" Didi barked at the young man.

"What?"

"Don't waste time, Trent. Tell him what you were doing here."

"No mystery. I get a hundred bucks for three bags of dirt from down there."

"That's it?" Brasco retorted. " A nice old lady tries to blow you away just for doing that? Who do you think you're kidding!"

Trent Tucker shrugged. "All I can do is show you."

The detective grabbed the young man roughly. "Let's go."

As he walked, Trent looked back over his shoulder at Didi. "Remember what I told you," he said.

"What do you mean?"

"Like I said, it ain't pretty."

She smiled sadly at him. "I see more bloody tragedies during one calving season than you can imagine exist."

The three of them walked down into the root cellar, Trent Tucker leading the way.

There was nothing out of the ordinary down there. The cellar, with its low ceiling, was a cold damp space with mounds of dirt that the wind had blown in over the years.

"I took a lot of dirt out of here, and there used to be a lot of broken glass jars," Trent whispered.

"Why the hell are you whispering?" asked Brasco as they crossed the room.

"The elevator keeps going down," Trent said. Then he walked to one wall and butted it with his shoulder. Afterward, he simply stood there looking at the wall. Didi and Brasco exchanged glances—as if asking each other whether Trent was insane. But then he repeated the action . . . and the wall moved . . . and revealed a perilously narrow and decrepit descending staircase.

"Watch your step," Trent warned the other two.

Didi counted twenty-seven steps.

The descent ended suddenly in a large, low-ceilinged space, triple the size of the root cellar above.

Trent suddenly flicked his beam off.

"Hey! What the hell are you doing?" said Brasco.

"There are lights hooked up down here," Trent replied. Then he vanished into the center of the dark space.

The lights came up and Didi began to survey the place. There were three naked overhead bulbs, spaced about five feet from one another.

There were old bunks along the wall, and a long table of pitted unfinished wood.

At the far end of the space was an old kiln.

Didi's eyes went to the floor of the space.

She brought her hand to her face in horror. She reached out to a wall to steady herself.

Five bodies!

They had been dead for a very long time. The faces and hands were shriveled, almost mummified. The tattered clothes were alien, bizarre-looking.

Two black males. One black female. Two white males. All twisted and touching in a macabre dance.

All she could think was that they had died in some kind of agony.

"Lord . . . Lord," Brasco said in a hushed voice. "What *is* this?"

"How do I know?" Trent Tucker said belligerently. "All I do is take the dirt out. I told you it wasn't pretty."

Suddenly Didi felt quite calm. There was something familiar about the scene. Something she had heard about or learned about a long time ago. She couldn't get a handle on it . . . but it was there . . . oh yes, it was somewhere . . . and that calmed her.

Chapter 8

Mid-morning. Sunny. Uncommonly mild. They were seated in the red Jeep in the hospital parking lot.

"Are you sure she's in there?" Rose asked.

"Yes," Didi replied stonily.

"Are you sure she has the answers?"

"Yes."

"So what do we have to lose?"

"Only our ignorance."

"We need flowers maybe," Rose suggested.

"There's a gift shop run by the volunteers, just inside."

They walked into the hospital and purchased a strange-looking bouquet made up of weirdly colored flowers and ferns.

Ella Baker was in room 304. She was sitting up in bed. The left side of her head was elaborately bandaged. There was a cut on the bridge of her nose just below the spot where her eyeglasses rested.

Ella smiled when she saw the visitors with their bouquet.

Didi sat down on the side of the bed. Rose put the flowers into a makeshift vase.

"Did you get the kitten?" Ella asked Didi.

"Your kitten?"

"Yes."

"I don't understand."

"Someone will be delivering her to you."

"But why?"

Ella didn't answer. She played with the hem of the bedsheet, then said, "My head doesn't stop hurting."

Rose sat on the other side of the bed. "I guess this will set you back on the work for your thesis," she said sympathetically.

"Yes, it will," Ella replied.

"Were you close to finishing?"

"Yes. Very close."

Rose gave Didi a quick glance: Didi picked up on it. She knew what was going on. Rose was asking for permission to proceed . . . to set Ella Baker up for the kill . . . the exposure. It was as if they were going to play cops and robbers—with the whole good cop/bad cop routine.

Didi had no qualms about using deception to trap Ella. Let Rose try whatever she wants to try, thought Didi.

The trouble was, Didi hadn't the slightest idea what Rose was up to . . . which direction she was heading in. She just knew that Rose's questions about the thesis were not what they seemed. Surely Rose had no real interest in Ella's work.

Only one thing was sure. Ella Baker was as guilty as sin. But of what?

Didi gave an almost imperceptible nod.

Rose smiled at Ella. "Didi tells me your thesis is on the Weathermen."

"That's right. With an emphasis on the women in the antiwar movement—or at least those women who were prepared to use violent means."

Rose nodded. She looked at the bouquet. "They will not last long," she noted.

"I think they're beautiful," Ella affirmed doggedly.

"You know," Rose said, "I did a senior paper on the Weathermen in high school. Oh, it wasn't as in-depth as a Ph.D. thesis—like yours. Just a few pages long, with a pathetic few footnotes and a laughable bibliography. But I didn't use that term."

"What term?"

"Weathermen. I thought they were called the Weather Underground."

"The terms are interchangeable."

"Oh. Anyway, I didn't like them at all. At least what I read of them. All that craziness and violence and bombs. I'm more of a Gandhi follower. You can't fight violence with violence."

"Then how do you fight it?" asked Ella.

"With love."

"You were probably a very young child—a mere infant—during the Vietnam War. If you were even alive then. I'm a bit older," Ella said primly.

"Yes, I was young. But in high school I had a friend who admired those people, who helped me with my paper. In fact, she used to take me on a pilgrimage."

"A pilgrimage?"

"Yes. To that lot in the East Village where three of them blew up their house and themselves while making bombs in the basement. My friend's name was Carla, and we used to go to that delicatessen around the corner—the Second Avenue Deli—and have huge pastrami sandwiches. Then we'd walk a half a block to the shrine." Rose paused for a moment. "Well, it wasn't really a shrine—just an empty lot. Made empty by terrorists, you could say."

"Yes, I've been there often," Ella said, nodding in agreement.

Rose sat up straight. "Oh, have you now?"

She then turned to Didi and smiled. "Well, you were right, girlfriend. Ella Baker is a full-blown liar. I don't know what or who she's doing this so-called thesis on, but it sure as hell isn't the Weathermen."

Ella looked at Rose, the blood draining away from her face.

"The house they blew up," Rose said, "was in the West Village—Greenwich Village—not the East Village. On *West* Eleventh Street."

Ella's voice came back at them in a low harsh whisper: "Get out of here . . . both of you."

Didi leaned over, very close to Ella's ear. "Silence won't help you. Patricia Napier is in custody. She is going to talk. You are going to be implicated in Jeremy Lukens's murder."

"You idiots!" Ella screamed. "Napier will

never say a word! And I didn't murder anyone!"

"Who are those people lying beneath the Magruder house?"

Ella looked around wildly. She did not answer. She tried to get out of bed but was too weak. She slumped back.

Didi kept up the pressure. "I know you distributed those Baggies with the hundreds in them. I know that the Baggie placed on your door made you afraid . . . made you run. We know now that you lied about your thesis. What else have you lied about? What else have you done, Ella?"

"You don't understand," she answered, desperate.

"No. Explain it to me."

"There wasn't supposed to be bloodshed. It all spun out of control."

"What spun out of control? What are you talking about? There was blood all over your front porch and yard—Jeremy's blood. Is that what you mean by 'spinning'? Three shots into his chest at close range, Ella!"

Ella raised her hand as if asking for mercy . . . or time . . . or understanding.

Didi and Rose waited without speaking.

Ella fumbled with the plastic water jug on the table next to the bed. Then she began to speak quickly, quietly—so quietly that Rose and Didi had to lean forward in order to hear.

"Buster Purchase knew he was going to die. He planned his suicide in a way where there would be a suspicion of murder.

"Above all he had to make his own death gruesome and perplexing enough to excite media attention.

"I got the snake venom for him, from my brother in California . . . from the Mojave. A young man named Bottoms held a squirrel against the greenhouse window, got mamma cat crazy, and she scratched Buster, which is what he wanted her to do.

"Then he spread the venom on the cat's claws and in his own wounds and staggered out to the bedroom to die in front of all those people.

"What killed him, though, was his bad heart, and the coronary he induced by swallowing a massive dose of amphetamines during the kitten auction. Oh, he had it planned down to the last moment!"

Didi could no longer restrain herself. "What

was the point of it all? If he decided it was time to die, why not just do it simply?"

"You don't understand. His death had to be coordinated with the opening of his shrine."

"Shrine? What shrine?"

"The shrine that was the Fat Man's dream. Buster Purchase considered himself much more than a jolly fat weatherman guy. He wanted to be remembered—to be taken seriously. He wanted to be given credit for finding it . . . excavating it. He wanted people to come to Hillsbrook on a kind of pilgrimage and enter the Buster Purchase Memorial Underground Chapel."

"Are you talking about those long-dead people underneath the Magruder house?"

"Yes. Two of them were fugitive slaves. One of them was a Negro freeman who betrayed them. The other two were white bounty hunters. What really happened down there one night in the 1850s is not clear. But it was violent and no one got out alive. It is, in total, a remarkable preservation. An unequaled find."

"You are *not* saying the Magruder farm was a stop on the Underground Railroad!"

"Yes. Yes, I am. In fact, that was what my

thesis was really about—the Underground Railroad in New York State. I was the one who told the Fat Man that if he was looking for the glory of discovery—and he always was—he should excavate the Magruder farm."

Didi tensed. She now knew why she had a sense of familiarity with that scene beneath the Magruder farm. All children who grow up in the Hillsbrook area are told the story of the network of cellars and secret rooms that were used to hide the fleeing slaves. They came up from the South through Pennsylvania, where the Quakers hid them, then across the southern tier of New York State, where the Moravians hid them, and then across Dutchess County on the way to New England and freedom. The town historians always bragged about the fervent abolitionist sentiment in the area. She had also learned that there was other sentiment in the area, Copperhead, pro-slave, particularly on the west side of the Hudson. And she had learned as a child about those bounty hunters of long ago who made a great deal of money apprehending the fugitive slaves. But as a child she really wasn't interested in that stuff so much. What she was really interested in was the ghost stories. Stories about those long-hidden cellars, which harbored the spirits of the escaping slaves, many of whom died in those cellars. Their spirits were dangerous, oh, very dangerous. Mrs. Tunney had even informed Didi that such a subterranean space existed beneath the Nightingale house. But, Mrs. Tunney had added, heaven help the person who finds it. Why had she forgotten all this? How strange it was!

Didi literally barked the next question at Ella: "Did you first meet Buster in Hillsbrook?"

"Oh no. I'm a friend of Sissy's from California. I met him when they first married, out there. I came east at his request."

"To coordinate the excavation?"

"To run it. And to do it secretly. To enlist young men in the area to do the digging. As more and more it seemed that the Magruder farm would be an astonishing find, Buster became more and more excited.

"Now he needed someone to coordinate the opening of the tomb with his flamboyant suicide qua murder . . . to deal with the press . . . to give structure to the event. He chose Jeremy Lukens and he sent Sissy to seduce him. Jeremy fell head over heels in love—like a silly schoolboy. He followed instructions. He opened a secret bank account. He made preparations for what Buster laughingly called a doubleheader: the suicide and the unveiling."

"Did Sissy do all this willingly?" asked Didi.

"She loved the Fat Man. She knew he was very ill. If he'd told her to jump off a moving train, she'd have done it. She tried to talk him out of it, of course—out of the whole lunatic scheme. But his mind was made up. He was fixated on it. He was going to die soon because of his heart, no matter what else happened, so he wanted to die his own way. He wanted to be remembered—not only as a chubby clown who did the weather on the West Coast."

"Why wasn't the shrine unveiled? Why did Jeremy hesitate? I mean, most of the place was excavated."

"After Buster's death, Sissy lost heart. She wanted out of here. She wanted out of the scheme. She was sick of Jeremy. She was appalled at how she had participated in her husband's conspiratorial death. She just woke up.

Fast. A few minutes after the Fat Man croaked. Sissy woke up and ran.

"But before she left she told me to inform Patricia Napier of the existence of the shrine on the property."

"What does Mrs. Napier have to do with all this?"

"Nothing, really. Except that the two slave-catching bounty hunters underneath the ground were her great-great-grandfather and his brother. And Sissy reasoned, correctly, that Patricia wouldn't like the world to know that the clean 'old money' in Hillsbrook came from hunting down fugitive slaves. She was ashamed."

"So what happened?"

"Not what we expected. You *saw* what happened. He died in your arms. I imagine Patricia Napier asked Jeremy not to open the tomb. He refused. She killed him."

Didi took some of the water for herself. It now made sense that Patricia Napier had tried to kill Trent. The Baggie delivered to her by Rose signaled that the scheme hadn't ended with Jeremy Lukens's death. The vault was going to be opened by persons unknown. She had to stop them too.

"There are a few things I really don't understand," Didi said. "For one, why did Buster have that kitten auction for a committee to save the Magruder farm, when such a committee already existed and was very well funded?"

"For Buster, the auction was the perfect milieu to die in. And I suppose he wanted it as a cover for the digging. If a committee was about to be established, activity on the property was logical. Of course, he wanted people to think it would simply be a restoration of the barn area—not an excavation of the foundation of the house. He couldn't disclose the existence of the committee because the money in there was being used on the clandestine excavation . . . to fill the Baggies with hundred-dollar bills . . . and to make Jeremy happier.

"The Fat Man might also have intuited that Pat Napier would go crazy if she knew what was down there. Getting her involved in the auction and the bogus project meant he could keep an eye on her.

"But look! When Sissy asked me to speak to Patricia Napier I never in a million years thought such a horror would happen. Who gives a damn how one's great-great-grandfather accumulated income? We're alive today—now. We're not responsible for something that happened a hundred and fifty years ago."

"And the lynx?"

"What about the lynx?"

"Buster told me it was a Michigan bobcat."

"He was probably just protecting the Bottomses—old and young. They helped Buster out. They provided a place where Sissy could seduce Jeremy and get him to help the Fat Man. They helped in the distribution of the bags. Sure, Carey Bottoms trapped a lynx for Buster. And Buster in turn told everyone it was a Michigan bobcat. Why he decided on raising hybrid kittens to auction never made too much sense to me. But the Fat Man, may he rest in peace, was always doing crazy things."

A pall of exhaustion settled on the three figures on the bed.

"It's kind of sad, don't you think?" Rose finally remarked. "The Fat Man's suicide via venom and amphetamines worked flawlessly. And then the whole plan unraveled immediately. The media spent about fifteen minutes on the death and then, so long. The wife co-conspirator panicked and ran. The designated promoter was murdered. And the Buster Purchase Memorial Museum—or whatever he called it—may never open. If it does, no one will connect it to the Fat Man, only to Magruder—and Patricia Napier."

Didi waved a hand in opposition. "You can put it another way, Rose. One live lunatic canceled out one dead lunatic."

"You mean Napier?"

"Yes."

"No!" It was Ella Baker who objected. "It *is* the saddest story, but Jeremy Lukens is at the center of it. All he had to do was accede to Patricia Napier's wishes that he forget about the shrine. Surely he saw the anguish in her request. Why didn't he drop it? After all, the Fat Man was dead. The woman he loved was gone. He really had no personal commitment to bringing this terrible part of history to light.

"Yet he refused. And so he died. Was it loyalty to the Fat Man's memory? Or the sudden discovery of a conscience—the emergence of some kind of duty to tell the truth about an episode from history? Just what made him do as he did? It's all so sad because he didn't have to die."

Rose noticed that the flowers had already begun to wilt. But she kept it to herself.

"I once read an essay," Didi mused. "It was translated from the French. The author said that in the court of Louis the Fourteenth the most witty, the most musical, and the most dangerous courtiers were fat men with bad hearts and ravenous sexual appetites."

"I can assure you," said Ella, "that Buster Purchase, by the time he moved to Hillsbrook, had no sexual appetites at all."

"No matter," Rose commented. "Hillsbrook is not Versailles."

"You are a disgrace! A disgrace!" Mrs. Tunney screamed at Charlie through the rolled-up window of Ike Badian's truck. She was wearing only a housecoat and seemed oblivious to the cold.

"I hate to send you out there, Charlie, but I gotta get back to my cows."

"Yeah. Okay," Charlie said, but he made no move to get out of the pickup. Instead he just slumped deeper into his seat and tried to ignore the enraged old woman on the other side of the glass.

Mrs. Tunney vanished for a minute. She had

found the Samurai costume in the bed of the truck. When she returned to the window, she was holding it up and trumpeting even louder: "Shame on you, Charlie Gravis! Shame on you!"

"She's yelling like you dressed up in a woman's clothes. Maybe she thinks you were impersonating a geisha," Ike noted.

"You're a jailbird now, Charlie," Mrs. Tunney shouted. Then, disgusted, she flung the costume down, stomped on it, and rushed back into the house.

"I'll get out in a minute, Ike."

"Look, Charlie. I'm sorry. It was all my fault. I should have figured that to invite in a bunch of old cowmen and feed them a couple of bottles of beer and then wave a fake cow with red udders at them—well, I should have known they'd act up."

"No, it was a conspiracy. They came to start trouble. They had a pail of milk with them, Ike. Did you tell Jack Randolph about the skit?"

"Yeah, I guess I did. But who would have figured?"

"The past has come back to haunt us, Ike."

"What the hell does that mean?"

"I don't know. But it sounds good."

"By the way, Charlie, how were my moos?"

"A thing of beauty," Charlie replied. Then he slowly climbed out of the vehicle to face the music.

Burt Conyers had stationed himself in front of the red Jeep. The two women approached.

"We're tired, Burt," Didi said. "We've no time for your games."

"Games? Me, play games? You mock me. But it is I who should mock you. Isn't it true that you never knew the Underground Railroad went right through and under Hillsbrook? Isn't it true that you never had the slightest inkling that Sissy Purchase had seduced Jeremy Lukens and driven him mad with love? Isn't it true that you never knew that Patricia Napier's money came from bounties on the heads of poor souls?"

He chuckled, grinned, spat, waved his staff, did everything but execute a gleeful dance.

Then he continued, "But look. I shall calm the waters. I shall write a poem about the Fat Man. I shall call him Abelard. And another poem about the beautiful young woman who prostituted herself for him in order to fulfill his dying wish. I shall call her Héloïse."

Rose waved her hand scornfully at the bearded man. "Are you telling us that you knew what was going on all along?"

He bowed. "But of course. I smelled it. It was in the air. I'm a weatherman as well as a poet. I always know which way the wind is blowing."

Nine minutes past midnight. Didi couldn't sleep. She had vacated the bed in favor of the rocking chair. The kitten Bernadine had, with some difficulty, gotten up and taken her place on the bed.

"You want to play musical chairs?" Didi asked her.

On the small table next to the bed were the remains of Didi's supper: New York State apples and New York State extra-sharp cheddar cheese.

Didi rocked and watched the kitten. Would Ella want her back? Why instruct her neighbor to send Bernadine to Didi, anyway? Just because she had extracted a staple from a cat's paw?

There was a full moon outside. It was a cold clear night. The beams came through the window and rested on the rug between the rocker and the bed.

She rocked herself grimly for about thirty minutes, and then fell into a troubled sleep on the chair.

The phone woke her about one in the morning. It was Allie Voegler, calling from Cooperstown.

Didi groaned, stretched, and then asked: "Are you drunk?"

Allie exploded with anger. "Why the hell would you make that assumption? What's the matter with you?"

"Calm down. When you used to call me at one in the morning, you had always had too much to drink."

"I haven't had a drop. I called to congratulate you."

"What for?"

"Brasco called me a couple of hours ago. He told me you were stupendous. He said you cracked Ella Baker like she was an egg from a free-running chicken. He says you cleared up everything."

"It wasn't that simple, Allie."

"And he said that idiot Trent Tucker was involved."

"Only peripherally."

"He said Charlie Gravis was in the lockup overnight."

"So Mrs. Tunney told me."

"Brasco said you took him down underneath the Magruder farm. Said there's a whole bunch of dead runaway slaves down there."

"Three, to be precise, Allie. Actually two, and a freedman. And two dead bounty hunters."

"Wild! It's about the wildest thing I ever heard."

"It *is* strange."

"But the thing I really can't absorb, Didi, is the notion that sweet Patricia Napier was wandering around Hillsbrook with a big ugly old .45 caliber World War Two army vintage sidearm blowing holes in people."

She didn't reply.

"And I find it hard to believe that the Fat Man killed himself to coincide with the opening of a root cellar, no matter how many old corpses they found in it, and no matter what the color of the corpses was."

She didn't answer.

"Are you sure you didn't miss a financial angle to the suicide, Didi? Some kind of insurance policy? Some kind of scam? Some kind of real estate deal?"

"Listen, Allie! It had nothing to do with money. Nothing! Buster had a small fortune. It was about him dying. And about his obsession. He didn't want to die a TV clown. He wanted his name to be remembered as the excavator of a real piece of Americana. He just didn't realize that there was a person in Hillsbrook who had an even stronger obsession. Patricia Napier had to make sure that crypt would never be opened. She was willing to do anything—even murder—to make sure that no one ever knew her family's wealth and status came from bounty hunting. Get it, Allie? Nothing in this whole mess was about money except the hundred-dollar Baggies for hungry farm boys. And maybe the bounty hunting itself. Maybe Patricia's great-grandfather didn't give a damn who they had to apprehend. It was one of the few ways to make a lot of hard cash then. Maybe a lot of old families made their money that way. Maybe a lot of old families worked both sides of the fence. Who knows? It was a long time ago, Allie. But in a sense the old cliche came true. The past haunts us. In this case it did more than haunt—it sent the Fat Man to a premature death, it murdered Lukens, it almost killed Trent Tucker, and it's going to send Patricia away for the rest of her life."

Allie was silent for a long time. They could hear each other breathing.

"Did I wake you?" Allie finally asked.

"Sort of."

"Okay. I just had to speak to you."

"Fine. Good to hear from you, Allie."

"One more thing."

"Yes?"

"Brasco told me Jeremy Lukens was having an affair with the Fat Man's wife."

"That's true."

"She was a beautiful woman."

"I agree."

"Brasco says the love deranged Lukens. He drew all kinds of strange sex pictures."

"Those I didn't see."

Allie laughed. "What if I told you that I did the same thing . . . when I fell in love with you."

"I'd say you were lying, Allie Voegler. Because you can't draw at all."

"Do you think my love for you is deranged?"

"I didn't know our current relationship was about love."

"Then you're a fool."

"That is possible."

"I think about you all day every day. That's all I talk about with the shrink—you. That's the only thing I look forward to—you. That's the only reason I have to beat this thing—you."

"What thing?"

"The suspension."

"Maybe you ought to stop fantasizing about me and start focusing on your problem."

"I got no problem, lady, except the absence of you."

Didi fell silent.

"We are going to be together again. I know it. I feel it. I can see it. In Hillsbrook. I can see you going out on rounds in that Jeep of yours. I can see myself waiting for you at the diner. I can even see myself getting along with Mrs. Tunney. I see it all."

Didi stood up and stared out the window. The moon had vanished. It was very dark.

"Do you hear me, Didi?"

"Yes, I hear you."

"Sleep good." He hung up.

The kitten was now in a ferocious battle with one of the pillows. Didi went to the bed, shooed her off, and lay down. The kitten struggled up again and sat down right beside her. Didi pulled gently at one of her ears. These hybrids, she knew, would never become domesticated. The first moment they had a chance to escape confinement, they would. They would end up feral.

The word feral seemed to capture her imagination. She reflected on the word. In a sense, Napier had become feral. And in a sense, Allie Voegler had always been feral.

She had a sudden desire to play some Patsy Cline, but the thought of those bodies under the Magruder farmhouse stanched the desire. So long dead, but never at rest.

She thought of the Fat Man—Buster Purchase. She could recall vividly that moment in the diner when he had suddenly appeared festooned in his ludicrous thousand-dollar imitation of a sheepherder's coat, and asked her to vet the hybrid kittens. She had always thought of him as a pathetic rich buffoon with a cultural yen. But no more. Tragic. He was tragic, not pathetic. Theatrical, but not a buffoon. Perhaps if she knew she would be dead in a day, a week, or a month, she would seek out a flamboyant exit. Perhaps she too would search out something or someone to attach to her name, so that people would remember Deirdre Quinn Nightingale as a great voyager or discoverer—not only as a country vet scratching out a living amidst rapidly diminishing cow herds.

No! No! She recanted. She was proud of her profession. She was not grandiose. She was not a megalomaniac. But one day, she knew, she must seek out that hidden chamber Mrs. Tunney swore was beneath the Nightingale house—deep beneath it.

The kitten climbed up on her chest. Didi smiled. Allie was in Cooperstown, and he claimed he loved her. Bernadine was in her bed and claimed she loved her. The elves below were all safe in their rooms, asleep. Except for her cash flow problem, things now were really not that bad.

Don't Miss the Next Book
in the Dr. Nightingale series:

*Dr. Nightingale Seeks
Greener Pastures*

Coming to you from Signet
in 1999

Deirdre Quinn Nightingale, D.V.M., sat primly on a bench in Philadelphia's 30th Street Station.

She had left Hillsbrook at eight in the morning, boarded a train to Penn Station in Poughkeepsie; changed for the train to Philadelphia; and was now waiting for a connection to Atlantic City.

It was just past noon, on an unseasonably warm March day.

Young Dr. Nightingale was dressed in purposefully severe fashion—charcoal gray business suit with a longish skirt—because she was headed for the Eastern States Veterinary Convention and it was important that she look her age . . . almost thirty.

It was a bitter fact of life for her that sometimes she was still carded when ordering a drink in places where she was not known. The doctor was pretty and exceptionally slight, with short-cut dark hair. These facts of her existence always made for age confusion, particularly when she was working in the field and attired in her usual outfit: well-worn overalls or jeans. In short, Dr. Nightingale sometimes looked like a little girl.

This was the first professional meeting she had attended in almost four years, and only the third since she had left vet school. But she was not treating the trip as a getaway—a much-deserved vacation. No, the reason for attending this conference was an altogether practical one.

Dr. Nightingale, in a hard-nosed look at the facts, had acknowledged that her veterinary practice was failing.

There were simply too few dairy farms remaining in Dutchess County. The cows had abandoned her.

She realized she had only two options if she wanted to go on in her profession, keep her house, her property, her animals, and provide a roof over the heads of the four elves (a motley collection of household retainers) she had inherited from her late mother.

Option number one: Expand the small animal practice—dogs, parakeets, kittens, and so on.

Option number two: Hook up with one of the big new breeding stables in the area, the ones that raised thoroughbred horses.

The first option was the more intelligent, of course, but Didi simply had no interest in being a small-animal vet.

The second choice intrigued her. Horses had long been a passion of hers. She went for this option. The trouble was, her experience in the field was meager (especially with race horses) even if her talents were great. And she was simply not up-to-date in equine medicine.

She needed to master the hottest new vocabulary of equine diagnosis and treatment. That is why she was waiting for the choo-choo train to take her to the convention at Atlantic City where, presumably, she would find out what was new and make some valuable contacts for getting work in this area.

Actually, during the four-day convention Didi would be sleeping thirty miles south of Atlantic City in the small seaside resort town of Cape May. The convention committee had reasoned, correctly, that many veterinarians probably didn't care for casinos and casino culture. So alternate accommodations were being offered—in Cape May, which was noted for its attractiveness to watercolorists, antiquers, and birdwatchers. Dr. Nightingale was not really interested in any of those activities, but she certainly found them all more appealing than gambling.

The convention . . . with its many exhibits by pharmaceutical companies, electronic imaging companies, and pet food conglomerates . . . and all the lectures and scholarly meetings were to be conducted at the brand new Atlantic City convention center on the boardwalk.

The loudspeaker in the 30th Street Station announced the boarding of New Jersey Transit train number 806 bound for Atlantic City—gate number five.

Didi picked up her leather attaché case and her aged valise with the leather straps around it, and headed for the gate.

By one-thirty she was registering at the convention center. She received her ID badge, the thick convention program, and confirmation of her bed-and-breakfast reservation in Cape May.

By two o'clock she was on the minibus, headed south. By two-thirty she was ensconced in her room, which was quite charming. It had a shower, but the bathroom was down the hall. The inn was a lovely old frame house with a wooden swing on its porch. It was only two blocks from the ocean, and she could hear and smell the breakers from her open window.

After unpacking, Didi sat on the bed and carefully went through the convention program, checking off meetings, seminars, and lectures she wished to attend.

The first "must" lecture was scheduled for late the next morning. The speaker would be Eleazar Wynn, a very successful racing vet. Didi had heard him speak before, in her last year of vet school. He was an impressive man. Tomorrow's topic would be "Lameness in the Rear Leg: New Problems, New Procedures."

Oh yes, that was definitely a must.

There was a knock at the door. Didi looked up, a bit startled. Was someone calling on her so soon after her arrival? And, more to the point, who could it be? She didn't know a soul in the area. Another knock. She walked over to the door and opened it.

"Hello! I'm your neighbor, Ann Huggins. Are you here for the EVA convention?"

"Yes."

"Good! So am I!"

The young woman in the doorway had an explosive, staccato way of speaking. In addition, she was, frankly, strange looking: at least six feet tall, stooped, with stringy yellow hair and very bright green eyes over which were bold patches of eye shadow. She was dressed in denim head to toe. For some reason she reminded Didi of the old R&B song "Mustang Sally."

"I hope you won't consider me a pest, but could you do me a favor?" the big blonde said. "A big favor! I mean . . . well, where the hell is the town of Cape May?"

Didi was startled by the question, perplexed. "You are in the town of Cape May," she replied. "You're standing in that town now." But then, she suddenly understood the meaning of Ann Huggins's question. "Are you talking about stores and such—shopping?"

"Yes! Yes, exactly. Stores."

"If you give me five minutes, I'll show you," Didi said, then added, "My name is Deirdre Quinn Nightingale, by the way."

"Ha! What a mouthful that is! What do people call you?"

"Didi, mostly. A few people just call me Nightingale."

"I like Nightingale. I'll call you that. You in private practice?"

"Yes. I work in Hillsbrook. That's Dutchess County, New York."

"Well, *again*, we're neighbors—almost. I'm from Toronto. You get ready; I'll be downstairs waiting." And with that she was gone.

Didi wondered how—why—anyone could consider Toronto to be "almost" the neighbor to Dutchess County. This tall blond woman with the piercing voice *was* a bit strange.

She closed the door, finished looking through the convention brochures, then went downstairs.

"I was here in Cape May once before, a few years ago," Didi explained as she led Ann Huggins away from the inn. "And if I recall, the main shopping area is only three blocks from the ocean, but you have to reach it circuitously."

"That doesn't make sense."

"I know it doesn't seem to. But it's true. You have to follow the contours of the hills, not the streets. This town is essentially built on dunes." Didi stopped there, realizing that instead of clearing up the confusion, she was just being more obscure. But within five minutes she had navigated them into the center of town—actually a village mall consisting of several fetching, red cobblestone streets where vehicular access was severely restricted. There were restaurants and shops of all kinds; many street vendors and performers; and plenty of benches to rest on.

"At this moment, Dr. Nightingale," Ann Huggins announced, "I have two powerful desires. A grilled cheese and bacon sandwich is the first. And a new pair of running shoes is the second. Will you allow me to treat you to one of the former as thanks for your yeoman directional help?"

"Sure," Didi agreed. "I'm hungry."

They each had an absolutely delicious grilled sandwich in a hamburger place called the Broasted Bun. During the repast, Mustang Sally revealed that she was a partner in a successful dog and cat clinic in Toronto and was really at the convention only to "play."

"Does that shock you?" She eyed Didi teasingly.

"No. In fact, I find it laudable. Unfortunately, right now I have other fish to fry."

"Well, you go and fry them good," Ann counseled. She finished her sandwich and compulsively cleared the table of crumbs, all the while expanding on what her Toronto establishment provided for clients and patients: surgery, kennels, grooming, testing, adoption services, in-patient and out-patient services, a retail shop for pet supplies, dietary supplements, and so on. Didi was properly impressed. Then Ann Huggins ordered coffee and apple crumb pie.

"You may find this difficult to believe, Nightingale, but I find male veterinarians sexy."

Didi hardly knew how to respond. All she could think to say was, "I was head over heels for one once."

"What happened?"

"He dumped me."

"Oh. Well, I never said they were nice . . . or bright. Only that I find them sexy. I don't know—they have a kind of goofy mixture of innocence and venality. You know what I'm saying?"

"Sort of," Didi replied, but she really didn't.

When they exited the restaurant the daylight was beginning to fade, the wind was up, and there was a hint of rain. More than a hint, actually. Several sea-laden drops landed on them. It really rained on the South Jersey shore.

"I am going to get those running shoes or die!" Ann Huggins exclaimed. "But I've imposed upon you enough. Please feel free to abandon me in my hour of need. Without remorse."

Didi laughed. She was beginning to like Ann Huggins.

"No," she said. "I'll take a look with you."

They found a perfect source two blocks away. The small store was chock full of athletic shoes and gear but seemed a bit quirky. The window display featured nothing but bedroom slippers.

"I definitely do not want one of those chain stores," Ann remarked.

"Then here you are. This place seems to be very non-chain," Didi answered, realizing even as she said it that this strange young vet had a way of eliciting irrational comments from her.

The store was long and narrow. On one side,

up and down the wall, sneakers and running shoes of all shapes, colors and functions were displayed.

On the other side was a long row of benches where customers might sit and try on their prospective purchases. Between the benches were free standing mirrors in which they could evaluate and admire themselves in their selections.

In the center—more or less dividing the deep room—were artfully piled boxes; it took Didi a few minutes to realize that this was not just a decorative display but the store's actual merchandise—the stock. There was something rather chic about the arrangement.

"Look at these!" Ann exclaimed in wonder, picking up one shoe.

It was a woman's running shoe, on sale for $107.95, regularly priced at $124.95.

The uppers were purple; the lowers were gray; and the bottoms were white. The shoe's leather laces were intricately twined.

Ann Huggins kept examining the shoe, turning it this way and that in wonder. "Actually, I don't run," she confessed.

Didi noticed the salespeople for the first time. One man was seated on the bench at the back of the store reading a newspaper. Another, a young Asian man, was fiddling with one of the boxes in the center aisle. He was watching Ann and Didi surreptitiously, trying to decide whether they were serious customers.

Didi looked toward the front of the store, where a customer was seated on one of the benches, staring down at an array of shoes on the floor. Obviously the poor man was having trouble making a decision.

Didi continued to look at him. She knew the man, she realized. But from where? From Hillsbrook? No, that wasn't it.

Of course! It came to her. That was Eleazar Wynn—the vet whose lecture she planned to attend. She had seen him only once before—years ago—but she remembered his distinctive, craggy face. There was no doubt about it; that was Wynn.

She turned back to Ann Huggins, intending to point out the famous vet to her. But Ann had moved deeper into the store, lured by the rack of shoes at the back.

Didi caught up with her.

"I've lost focus," Ann complained. "I've forgotten what the hell I was looking for in the first place."

"Running shoes," offered Didi.

"Yes! Yes, you're right. Thanks."

The salesman who had been so engrossed in the newspaper suddenly leaped out of his seat, the paper falling to the floor.

And the young Asian man was now shouting wildly.

Both men began to run toward the front of the shop.

Didi and Ann looked at each other in confusion.

"What is it? . . . What? . . . *What!*" Ann was looking around frantically.

Didi took off after the two running men, pulling Ann along with her.

The four of them formed a circle around the customer. Eleazar Wynn, who was dead, slouched in his chair. There was a long, pencil thin black object sticking out of the main artery of his neck. He had died within sixty seconds of being stabbed, without uttering a sound.

The sneakers he had been inspecting were now awash in blood. Bright red arterial blood. His.